PRETTY GIRLS NEVER LIE

SJ SYLVIS

AUTHOR'S NOTE

Pretty Girls Never Lie is the *last* book in the St. Mary's Series (but can be read as a standalone!). The St. Mary's Series is a **DARK** boarding school romance series intended for **MATURE** (18+) readers. This series is labeled as such due to the dark themes throughout. Be aware that it contains triggers that some readers may find bothersome. **Reader Discretion is advised.**

PROLOGUE

ISLA

Sobs rock my chest, but his hand around my mouth muffles each cry that tries to escape. My spine is unrelenting against his front when his arm flexes around my waist. I want to break through the closet door to stop what's happening through the tiny openings in between the blinds, but his warm breath ghosting my ear stops me.

"Don't do it, Isla," he warns.

My teeth clank together and chatter. I'm freezing but sweating at the same time.

"*Please.*" He's pleading with me, and there's a strange twisting in my belly that wants to give in to him even if he's practically a stranger.

I know nothing more than his name and the exact shade of green in his eyes, but I'm drawn to him like my father is to bad decisions.

I move against Brantley's arm, and his muscles flex. His voice is comforting, and I find myself clinging to it like he's my own personal safety net.

"He'll kill you if he sees you."

I swallow the lump in my throat. My eyes water at the sight of the gun pressed to my father's temple, and the second the trigger is pulled, I turn around and bury my face in the shoulder of my best kept secret.

Oh my god. Oh my god. Oh my god.

The cries of my younger brother echo through the house, and a gruff voice barks out a demand.

"Shut that fucking baby up, or I'll kill it too."

I gasp right before I feel a tug on my hair.

"Do not make a noise."

I can't decide if Brantley is trying to save me or himself, but it doesn't really matter. As long as I'm quiet, I'll live.

That's what he told me moments ago when he pulled me into the closet and slapped his hand over my mouth.

My head follows the jerking of my hair, and although it's near black in the closet, I try to make out his familiar features. I can only see an outline of his face at first, but as soon as my eyes adjust to the bleak darkness, I find the harsh angle of his jaw and his boyish messy hair.

He's near the same age as me–that much I do know from the first time he found me lurking. He called me a meddler and told me to go back to my bedroom. The second time he caught me, he *took* me back to my room, and the third time, he stayed.

I jump at the sound of the man outside the closet. "Where the fuck is Brantley?"

Brantley's arm tenses, and then he curses under his breath. "*Shit.*"

My younger brother is wailing from his bedroom, and I'm sick to my stomach.

I smell metal. The need to retch overtakes me, and I gag.

"Stop it," he hisses.

I clench my eyes shut when he pushes my face into his chest. His heart is flying faster than mine, and I can't help but wonder why. Is it because of what we witnessed, or is it because he's afraid his father is going to open the closet door and see him in here with me?

"Call Richard."

Brantley sighs at the conversation on the other side of the closet door.

"On it."

There are shuffling footsteps, and I freeze. *They're going to find us.*

A salty tear falls down my cheek, but Brantley is quick to wipe it away, flinging the moisture elsewhere.

There's silence, except for my brother's cry.

The gunshot woke him.

The gunshot that killed my father.

The gunshot that took away my only living parent.

What am I going to do?

"I have to go," he whispers in my ear.

I want to tell him to stay because I'm afraid, and the second he leaves, where does that leave me?

His hands drop from my shaking body. "He's looking for me, and if he finds out you exist and that I hid you, we're both as good as dead."

My whisper cracks through the stuffy closet. "What do I do?" I hardly recognize my voice.

"Become fucking invisible."

What?

"If he knows you exist and that you just witnessed…" his voice trails off. "Just…stay the fuck away from this life, okay? Disappear. Lie if you have to."

He shoves me aside, and I fall to my knees. My arms wrap around them like that's going to protect me from the unbearable future I'm about to find myself in.

It smells like blood.

My soft voice breaks through the tension. "My dad always told me that pretty girls never lie."

Brantley drops down to my level at the last second and takes my wet face in his hands. "If you want to live, you'll lie, Isla. Get your shit together, and remember that you're still alive. Don't make me regret saving you."

The closet door opens, and I peer up at him. His light-green eyes meet mine, and although his words were a bite to my skin, he gives me a look that I know I'll keep under lock and key forever. I smash my lips together, and then he's gone.

The closet door slides shut, and I sit with my knees trapped behind my arms and watch him through the tiny cracks.

"There you are." An older man enters the room. "Where have you been? Your father told me that you need to clean up this mess."

This mess? Does he mean my father's body? I shut my eyes to keep from looking at what lies beneath their feet.

"I've been here the whole time."

It's true.

He has been.

"Well, get this shit cleaned up so we can go. That baby is driving me up a fucking wall."

My lip quivers, but I refuse to let another tear fall.

My brother's wails are at an all-time high.

I freeze when those familiar green eyes fling to the closet door. For the next several minutes, I press the heels of my palms into my eyes and try to acknowledge that my life is forever changed.

ONE

ISLA

I crane my neck and stare at the stone with the sun pounding onto my back. I read the engraved lettering and sigh. *St. Mary's Boarding School.*

It looks like a castle.

Too bad I'm the furthest thing from a princess.

St. Mary's Boarding School is out for the summer, but I'm one of the less-fortunate students—or fortunate, depending on who you're talking to—that has been sent here to receive their high school diploma. I'm a few credits short, and it was either come here for summer classes or redo my senior year.

The choice was obvious, but Raven—my bossy, thinks-she-has-my-best-interest-in-mind social worker and newest school counselor—thinks she bullied me into coming. Technically, she isn't my social worker any longer since I'm eighteen and have voluntarily left the WITSEC program, but that doesn't stop her from meddling in my life.

"Are you ready?" she asks.

I block the sun with my hand and shoot her a look. That's the only response she's going to get today.

Raven's heels click against the stone as she climbs the steps, expecting me to follow after her. "I know you're frustrated, but you need a diploma, Isla."

I snort, causing her to turn toward me in a huff.

We're complete opposites. I'm an orphan who's been called trash more times than I care to admit, and she's probably never known what it's like to be lonely. Her jet-black hair is shiny, whereas my near-white blonde locks are dull and tangled. She wants to help others, and all I want is to help myself.

And Thomas.

"I told you I'd look for Thomas if you did this."

A sarcastic laugh leaves me as I climb the steps after her. I wait until I'm a foot from her when I say, "And that's the only reason I'm here." *What she doesn't know is that I'm already ten steps ahead of her.*

She shrugs, and a soft smile curves onto her face. "Bribery always works."

I roll my eyes and pull my worn backpack higher onto my shoulder. The heavy door opens, and I cringe at the expansive entryway. *Is this place fucking haunted?*

"Raven."

"Tate," Raven's voice is instantly breathy. She may be thin, but she's not *that* out of shape to be breathing hard from the few steps we climbed, so that tells me this man means something to her.

"It's…" He runs his eyes down her body before meeting her eyes again. "It's, uh…good to see you."

She clears her throat. "Same to you. I'm happy to see you've taken over and have given me this opportunity." Raven waves her hand out in front of her, gesturing to the sparkling white-and-black checkered floor. They both scan the area, and I can tell by the faraway look in both of their gazes that they're revisiting a memory.

An old fling? Hmm.

"Well, as interesting as this is…" Silence trails my sentence in an attempt to break them out of their awkward trance.

"Right, right!" Raven grabs me by the arm and pulls me farther into the boarding school. "This is Isla Ransford."

My eye twitches. My real last name was buried with my father the night he died, so Ransford is nothing but a reminder that I belong to no one.

"Hi, Isla. I'm Headmaster Ellison. It's so good to have you with us this summer."

My lips are glued shut, but the profanity that's occurring behind them would make my dead grandmother turn over in her grave.

"Raven and I have a few things to discuss about your academics and her newest position, but please feel free to go up the stairs behind me, and you'll find your new room. Your name is taped to the front of the door. There aren't many students here for our summer program, but I'm sure you'll make a few friends."

"I don't need friends," I admit, walking around him.

It's a cold thing to say, but the truth isn't always warm and fuzzy.

The headmaster doesn't seem fazed by my attitude in the slightest, so I'm interested to know what kinds of students have attended this boarding school in the past.

Probably none with issues like mine.

The wood railing is smooth against my palm as I climb the steps. I'm not eager to make this place a home, but it is one step closer to Thomas, so I'm a little less glum than before. As melancholy as this dark and moody school seems, I won't let it put a damper on the progress I've made over the last month.

I tuck my hair behind my ear and push on the door with

my name on it. I pray I don't have a roommate, because it'll only complicate things. The very last thing I need is some girl who thinks her life is terrible poking her head into my business, only to realize she has *no* idea what terrible is.

"It can't be."

My attention flicks to the shadow in the corner of the room, and I pause with one foot in the hallway and one right past the threshold. There's an uptick in my pulse, and something familiar whooshes through my brain. It's like a memory that's too hazy to see, but it makes you feel something anyway.

"Excuse me?" I scan him from behind. He's tall with shoulders so wide he blocks the sun from the window.

His chiseled jaw turns in my direction. "I thought I told you to become fucking invisible."

My lips part.

The feeling of dread plows into me so abruptly that I immediately take a step back into the hallway.

Become fucking invisible.

Those were some of his last words to me.

Yet here I am, appearing as tangible as the fear tethering me to the very boy who saved my life but ruined it all the same.

TWO

School seemed so trivial months ago. Other things–more pressing things–took precedence over an algebra test or the seven-page essay I was supposed to write to secure a passing grade, but now here I am, trying to obtain my diploma so I can get on with my life.

I exit out of the inmate search and slip my phone into my pocket. I know it's an unhealthy habit to continuously check that my father is still behind bars, but I do it anyway because it's part of my newfound freedom.

Though, how long will that really last? Who's to say he doesn't show up on my doorstep one day to kill me for turning on him? History can repeat itself. The name on the door behind my back is proof of that.

The dorm room is filled with nothing but a few measly pillows and a folded blanket at the end of the bed, but the moment the door opens, the space suddenly feels crowded.

Every nerve ending comes alive like a wildfire tearing

down a forest. I crack my neck and say the first thing that comes to mind.

"It can't be." *It's her. I know it's her.* I can feel it in my gut.

"Excuse me?" Her voice is the same besides the angry little edge to it.

I turn slightly and am shocked by how different she is. It's only been four years, but *fuck,* she's…pretty. "I thought I told you to become fucking invisible."

Her gasp cuts through the room, and it's almost as if I can feel her warm breath brush against my face. I push the memory of that night into the back of my head, trapping it there with the rest of the damage that was done to me over the years, and turn all the way around.

The door shuts in my face, and she's out of my sight. I heave in a breath and get my bearings together.

If I believed in God, I'd curse the fuck out of him right now. *Why is she here?* When I first saw her name on the white-board hanging on the door, I froze. There was no way it was the same girl I risked my life for, coming back to haunt me and remind me of everything I detested in my childhood. But with hair as white as snow and icy blue eyes, I know it's her.

It's Isla.

Isla *Ransford.* She may have a new last name, but it's still her.

My father always taught me to clean up my messes, and she was the one mess I didn't dare touch.

I silently prowl across the floor, but I know she can feel me coming for her. I rip open the door and meet her eyes head on. They're so frosty a burst of ice flies through my veins.

"Remember me?" I ask, running my gaze down her frame.

Her mighty chin is firm, and her eyebrows are furrowed with anger. She's filled out in places that I couldn't even conjure up in my head over the last few years, and I hate her for being soul-suckingly gorgeous.

"How could I ever forget you?" she spits.

I don't smirk, but my lips tingle all the same.

I want to tell her off and grab her by her perfect little throat to drag her out of this school, but my fists stay flexed at my sides, and my feet remain unmoving inside her new room. "You need to leave," I manage to say through the mess in my head.

Isla's light-pink lips curve into a crescent, and it takes me by surprise. It's crystal clear that she's being devious, and the twinkle in her eye sends something warm into my chest. *Oh, we like to play games now, do we?*

"I'm not leaving. Didn't you hear? I'm out of WITSEC because the past finally caught up with your pathetic father."

She was in WITSEC?

I force out a sarcastic laugh, and it irks her. I'm not even going to try to decipher why I enjoy the rise I get out of her.

"You say that now." I take a step toward her, and a weird sense of pride swells when she stays in the exact same spot against the red carpet-lined hallway. My hand finds its place on her little chin, and I squeeze it tightly. "Trust me when I say you'll be changing your mind after being trapped in a place like this…*with me.*" I shift my gaze to her light hair and blue eyes. "You're going to be begging to go back into WITSEC, *Goldilocks.*"

Isla rips her chin out of my grasp, and I chuckle.

I'm toying with her. Why am I toying with her?

"You think I'm afraid of you, Brantley?"

I raise an eyebrow. I wasn't sure if she remembered my name, but then again, I bet she remembers everything from that night.

"I don't think you're afraid of me." *But you will be if you don't get the fuck out of this school.* "Why would you be afraid of the guy who saved you?"

A sweet, melodic laugh floats throughout the empty hallway. "I hope you haven't spent the last four years thinking of yourself as a hero, because trust me when I say that you didn't save me at all."

"Keeping someone from killing you in cold blood isn't saving you?"

I hid her and kept my father from ever finding out that Amos had an older daughter, but she's right—I'm no hero.

Isla takes a step closer to me. Her sweet, sugary scent wraps around me and tricks me into thinking we're somewhere other than St. Mary's Boarding School. "You may have kept your psychotic father from killing me, but my life has been filled with nothing but torment since that night. If you think for one fucking second that you're my knight in shining armor, you're mistaken."

Damn, she's feisty.

And I like it.

Anger and pride swarm together and concoct one hell of a reaction. My hand cups the back of her head, and I pull on the strands of her thick waves. Her lips part, and her warm gasp lands on my mouth. "I've never considered myself a hero after that night. I know I'm a goddamn villain, which is why you shouldn't bother unpacking that measly little backpack you've thrown off to the side."

Isla pushes on my chest, and I let her go. She tumbles backward but gets her bearings quickly before she swoops down to gather her belongings. *One backpack? Really?*

"Get out of my way," she barks.

I move to the side and watch her stomp into her room with her back to me. The contents of her life spill onto the bed, and she shoots me a glare. "Leave."

I smile. "Only if you leave first."

THREE

Classes started three days ago, and the only thing that has done is irritate me because instead of spending my time following up on my younger brother, I'm stuck inside a classroom that reeks of dust and fake promises of a better future.

Not to mention the other ten students in the classroom and how they all stare at me like I'm an alien instead of a girl who failed her senior year of high school. But newsflash: they did too.

"Hey, Elsa."

I roll my eyes at the joke. I've been called Elsa more times than I can count.

Slowly, I spin on the black-and-white checkered floor and sigh at the sight of a guy close to my age. He's tall and has an emo look to him with jet-black hair and a piercing in his left eyebrow. His smirk is hot, but that's all he has going for him after referring to me as an ice queen.

"Nice joke," I say. "Very original."

I turn and begin heading back to my dorm until I feel a

hand on my hair. My head tilts backward with the gentle tug, and I bare my teeth when I catch the eye of my current admirer.

"Oh, come on. Gonna ice me out?"

His friend snickers, and my mouth parts with his stupidity.

"If you touch me again, I'm going to do much more than ice you out." I roll my eyes and huff with a turn, but then his hand lands on my arm, and I'm furious. I fling his fingers off my elbow right before I'm shoved backward by someone else.

"Who gave you permission to touch her?"

I stare at the back of Brantley's head. My finger twitches to shove his hat off and stomp on his foot at the same time. *How dare he act like my hero again!* There's an insult flying out of my mouth before I even realize what it is.

"And who gave you permission to break into my house and shove me into a closet, Brantley?"

When his green eyes meet mine, my pulse skips. A flash of that night strikes me like lightning, and my eyes fall to the floor. Thomas's cries fill my head, and I close my eyes to push the distant memory away.

When I feel a tight grasp against my upper arm, I snap to attention. My books tumble out of my arms and land on the floor, but I leave them as Brantley drags me through a nearby door, shutting out the rest of the school. I cough at the flying dust particles, and the smell of mildew burns my eyes.

"Who the fuck do you think you are?" he seethes.

I fight through the darkness to see him, but I can't. We must be in the janitor's closet or maybe some secret hideaway. I wouldn't be surprised in a fortress like this.

"Who the fuck do you think *you* are?" I snap back. My arms cross against my chest, and my heart thumps with thunderous beats against them. "I don't need you to come to my rescue!"

Brantley's chuckle warms my skin, but a cold chill races

down my back. I shiver at the sensation and ignore the dip in my lower belly. My thoughts are twisted, and memories are hitting me from every angle. I was forced to meet with numerous social workers, counselors, and therapists over the last four years to get a grasp on the past, but I can't deny the push and pull I've always felt when I thought of him. It's even worse after coming face to face with him again. There's a very vulnerable part of me that wants to rush into his arms, because as much as he is a part of that awful night, he *did* protect me, no matter how hard I try to paint him as the bad guy.

Fuck, fuck, fuck.

My legs tingle with fear, and I take a step backward. Something crashes to the floor, and a bang echoes throughout the tiny area. I yelp and jump at the same time. A gunshot distantly rings throughout my subconscious, and I try to escape the stark darkness.

I curse when my elbow hits something hard. I reach my hands out for the doorknob, trying to escape, but grab onto his shirt instead.

"For fuck's sake, what the hell are you doing?"

I gasp for air and turn around. "Let me out of here."

"No." Brantley's hands land on my waist, and he pulls me backward into his chest. His hot whisper coats my neck, and I freeze. "Not until you either leave this fucking place or keep your mouth shut." I focus on his heart pounding against my back. *Calm down, Isla.* "You think it's smart to go around and spew things about that night? In a place like this?"

"In a place like this?" My words are chopped between lungfuls of air, but I'm more grounded now that his hands are on me, which is so incredibly humiliating to my pride. "It's a fucking high school."

I gasp when I'm quickly spun around in his arms and slammed against his chest. The movement causes a dizzy spell to take over. The light flickers on, basking the small area with a warm glow. I blink until his handsome face is steady. He looks so much older than I remember, more rugged and sure of himself. The boyish vibe to him is replaced with something dangerous, and the rebellious part of me suddenly wants to play with fire.

"You have no idea what has happened in this *fucking high school*, Goldilocks. So shut *up*." His tone is lethal. "While you've been playing house in your comfy little witness-protection world, far away from men like my father, I've been *here*." I stay still when his hand snakes past my waist to land at my neck. I swallow against his palm and know that I should be afraid, but I'm not. "Never bring up that fucking night again. You got it?"

I dip my gaze down to his mouth. His kissable lips form a firm line, and anger radiates from his shoulders. There's a bratty rebuttal testing my ability to listen to him, but I think twice with his hand around my neck. "Then never step in and try to protect me ever again." I move closer to him and watch his eyebrows twitch with confusion. I grab on to his sturdy wrist that's holding me in place and lean forward. "You got it?"

Our mouths are a breath away, and I want nothing more than for him to lean in and press his lips to mine just so I can draw blood and prove to him that WITSEC was the complete opposite of what he's thinking.

"You think I'm protecting you, Isla?" he asks, tilting his head in the way that only a villain would. "I'm not protecting you. I'm protecting myself."

I almost fall forward when he rips his palm from my neck and pushes past me, leaving me all alone in a small closet for the second time.

FOUR

My phone is blowing up, but it's doing nothing to help distract me from the chaos I feel. What are the fucking odds that Isla is here? Is it karma? Is it fate fucking with me?

I grip my phone hard and try to focus on the texts.

Isaiah: Gem and I are going out to eat if you guys want to come.

Isaiah: She's going to drive, so there's a good chance we won't even make it, though.

Gemma: Rude.

Shiner: Avoid stone walls.

Cade: I bet Brantley wishes you'd hit the school so he could have an excuse to dip out of there.

Shiner: Poor Brantley. Stuck in summer
school. Should have focused on his studies a
little more.

I growl, but there's a hint of humor behind my anger.

Me: Sorry, I was too busy saving everyone's
girlfriends to focus on the fucking quadratic
formula.

Shiner: Don't get angry with me! I don't have
a girlfriend. I'm single and ready to mingle at
college, babyyyyy.

Collectively, we all text the same thing at the same time.

Me: Shut up.

Cade: Shut up.

Isaiah: Shut up.

Gemma is the only one who gives Shiner a sweet response, but that's just how she is. How she ever turned out the way she did, after her shitshow of a life, is beyond me. I was raised by a psycho, and I can feel him in my veins from time to time—and I know it's the same for my friends and their upbringings too.

I put my phone down and start pacing again.

St. Mary's is lonely without the Rebels here. Our senior year was filled with so much mayhem that my body doesn't know how to react without it. Nerves eat away at me, and my brain keeps attaching itself to the one thing that's sending my days into a disarray. Isla is taunting me, even if she doesn't realize it.

I throw my phone to the side and stomp over to my door. It takes me no more than a few seconds to walk over to the girls' hallway. During the regular school year, it's loud. There's usually girly chatter behind a cloud of hairspray, but now that everyone is gone, besides a handful of students, it's quiet.

I stand in front of her door. I could knock, but I use the element of surprise instead. I twist the doorknob and scoff when I realize the door is slightly ajar. Tell me you lived a cushy life in WITSEC without actually telling me. Only someone who hasn't had to watch their back every day of their life would leave their door unlocked in a place as expansive as St. Mary's.

Isla's sweet scent wraps around me when I search the room for her. I come up empty-handed and ignore the pang of disappointment that settles to the floor.

Fine, I'll wait.

I walk in farther and prepare myself for another spar because I know for a fact, she's going to be irate when she finds me in her bedroom. Anger skims the surface when I think about the last encounter we had. Red filled my vision when she mentioned that night in front of other people. What was she thinking? Is she *that* stupid? Doesn't she know that my father would kill her on sight if he knew she was alive and could ID him at a moment's notice?

Sure, he's in prison now, but she should have stayed hidden.

My father doesn't realize, or maybe he doesn't care, but I know he's putting a target on every last string that's tying him to more years behind bars. The Rebels and I have already discussed the logistics of our fathers' brains. We know how they tick, and we know they require silence in order to survive and be up for parole one day.

Apparently, Isla isn't as smart as I'd hoped if she's willing to make mention of that night.

My fingers brush over her pillow with the small indent from her head. I grind my teeth and shake the image of her lying on her bed from my thoughts. Her scent is even stronger the closer I get to her belongings, which aren't much.

I'll admit that I've thought of her over the years and wondered where she was, but that was only because I never thought I'd see her again. I allowed myself to revisit the vague memory of our quiet moments, hiding behind her bedroom door in an attempt to keep her from eavesdropping because I *knew* things would get hairy and she'd get caught in the crossfire.

I shake the memory away and walk over to her math book to pull out the Polaroid photo sticking out in between the pages.

I lose my breath with the blast to the past.

The girl staring back at me is the one I remember from my memories. Isla's blonde hair frames her face, and her innocent smile is so bright it sends a rush of warmth through my body. I drop the photo, like it's going to burst into flames in my hand, and stare at it from up above.

Her father looks a lot better in the photo than the last time I saw him. There's life in his eyes as he cradles his son in one arm with his other wrapped around his daughter.

Fuck.

I spin around and pinch the bridge of my nose.

The Rebels joke that I'm cold. I'm the stoic one of the group, in control and restrained, but the only reason I'm able to act that way is because I've honed the skill to block it all out.

Except, now there's a giant neon sign pointing in my direction and destroying every last wall with subtle reminders of the very beginning and everything *after*.

I freeze when the door pushes open and in walks my own personal ice princess.

The bun on top of her head that's full of her thick hair bounces when she stops abruptly. Her blue eyes harden, and I can't help but notice the way she crosses her arms over her perky breasts as a defense mechanism.

"What the hell are you doing in my room?"

Just like old times.

I lean back on her desk and cross my ankles. Pain bites my fingertips with the force I'm putting on the wood to hold myself back from storming over to her and demanding she tell me her reasoning for being here.

My voice is level and controlled, though I'm full of madness while looking into her eyes.

"Why are you here, Isla?"

Her face twitches with refusal. I prepare for a lie, but she takes me by surprise.

"To find my brother." Isla shuts the door behind her, and suddenly, I don't like that we're alone. "And I've decided that you're going to help me."

The fuck I am.

She's a foot away from me, and I fall right into her trap because my body feels something unfamiliar but addicting at the same time.

Shit, get away from me.

"After all, you do owe me, Brantley."

FIVE

His jaw ticks, and he leans away from me. I note the amount of space between us, and confusion lingers when I realize he is trying to add to it. I guess he only likes to be close to me when *he's* in control.

"I owe you?" Brantley shifts with a roll of his eyes. "You're out of your fucking mind, Ice Princess."

Ice Princess? I could handle him calling me Goldilocks, but princess is a hard no from me.

I instantly recoil. "I am the furthest thing from a princess."

Brantley is back to being sure of himself–hot, smug, confident. He talks with ease, and each syllable is smooth falling from his lips. "Let's see," he starts. I follow his slow movements and zero in on his thumb rubbing slowly over his chin. "Orphan, *check*. Damsel in distress, *check*. Needs a prince to help her, *check*." I freeze when he reaches up and hooks his finger underneath my hair tie. I jerk forward when he pulls on it, allowing my hair to fall down in one *whoosh*. "Thick, beautiful locks of hair, *check*." My cheeks flush, and I shove his hand away. "You seem like a princess to me."

"Fuck you."

Brantley smirks, and it should be illegal. I hate that my stomach bottoms out from the sight. "Wants to fuck the prince, *check.*"

My jaw flings open, and a hot gasp rushes from my mouth. "Oh my god. That is not true!"

I step backward when he leans on my desk again. He shrugs, and I become more unhinged the longer we're in my room together. The thought of scrapping the whole plan of him helping me is there, but my brother's fate is more important than my dignity.

I breathe through my nose and try again. "You can try to piss me off all you want, but you *will* help me."

Brantley flies off my desk and storms over to me. Out of surprise, I rush backward until I hit my door with a huff. His hand winds around my waist, and he pulls me into his chest to keep me from banging my head off the wood. "Who do you think you are, Isla? Coming to my school and demanding things of *me?* Shouldn't you be afraid of me?"

Afraid?

His hands are chains holding me captive.

"I can't decide if you're brave or stupid."

I tremble and hope he doesn't notice. "I prefer...determined." My words are no better. They clamor out of my mouth in a jumbled mess. "And I'm not afraid of you."

"You should be."

"That's twice you've said that, and I've yet to witness you do something that scares me."

I know I'm doomed the moment I watch the excitement blossom in his eyes. His mouth twitches, and it distracts me. One second, I'm pressed against his thundering chest, and the next, I'm cheek to door with his hands on my hips, holding me steady.

A hot, needy breath escapes my mouth when he heats my neck with his words. "Do you know how easy it would be for me to pin you against this door and fuck you, Isla? To take advantage of you and do things to you that you've never even dreamed of? To scar you so badly you never once think of asking for my help again?"

My heart pounds violently, and a chill ices my bones. But surprisingly enough, it's not out of fear. I've been held down by a man before, and this is not the same as a drunken foster daddy needing to cop a feel.

I turn my head so our mouths are almost touching. His brow furrows with his lips glistening from his tongue running along the crease. "You think this is the first time a man has held me down, Brantley?"

What is this? Stockholm syndrome? He's right. I *should* be afraid of him. I shouldn't react in this way and bait him like he's harmless. I know, deep down, that just because he saved me years ago doesn't mean he'd do it again. Brantley could do things to me that would send me running for the hills, but there's a catch that's making me hesitate. *A feeling.* A connection that I cannot even begin to explain.

Brantley's hands tighten against my waist with my revelation. There's a worry line in between his eyebrows, but he quickly hides the truth with another bite. "Oh, so you like to be afraid, then?"

My jaw clenches, but I stay quiet.

"You like the thought of me putting my hand around your neck and fucking you from behind, don't you?"

I start to breathe heavily, and there's a tug in between my legs. *No, what?* My bra suddenly feels too tight. The room narrows when Brantley's hand skims up my belly, and settles around my neck. His touch is gentle, but the meaning is heavy. My pulse rams against his palm like it's going to run right out of this room. I drop my eyes to his mouth, and his loud gulp fills the room when his fingers thrum against my skin.

"Your pulse is flying, Ice Princess. Are you afraid...or

turned on?" Brantley's head tilts. "Or are you turned on because you're afraid?"

"Why don't you find out?" I ask.

I am playing a dangerous game, and I know it.

Brantley's hand disappears, and a wall of cold air hits my back. I spin and watch him put much-needed distance between us. "You're not as stupid as I thought. You're… devious." His eyebrow rises. "I'm kind of proud."

Oh, shut up.

I open the door and wave my hand forward for him to leave. He says nothing when he passes by, and I don't breathe again until he's far enough down the hall to disappear out of my sight.

SIX

I am not helping Isla.

In fact, I'm staying clear the fuck away from her.

Never mind the fact that I'm watching her every move like a druggie that can't wait for their next fix, or that the second she walks into a room, my eyes find her, and my blood runs hot. I hate that it's difficult *not* to look at her.

I'm drawn to her, and I hate it.

"Brantley?"

I slowly shift my eyes from the back of Isla's head to the headmaster as he pops into the classroom. Everyone in the room turns to look at me—*except* her.

"Can you please come with me for a moment?"

Mrs. Carter chimes in, "And turn your test in before you go."

I glance down to the answers. I usually don't care about tests and homework, *but* considering all my friends are about to head off to college and I'm sitting in summer school, I actually put forth effort.

My strides are lazy as I walk in between the desks and absentmindedly brush Isla's arm. I smirk when she refuses to move it and keep the smirk plastered to my face until I'm in the quiet hall with the headmaster, who just so happens to double as a father figure to the Rebels and me.

"I have good news."

Headmaster Ellison looks like a kid in a candy shop. He's been that way ever since Gemma, to be honest.

"You found me a way out of summer school?" I reply.

His brows furrow. "No. But it does require you to graduate. Tell me you actually studied for that test, Brantley."

I roll my eyes. "I did."

"Good, because you can put a pinky amount of effort in and probably get an A. You're smart."

I turn my head at the compliment. It makes me itchy.

"What do you need, Tate?" I act bored, but I am interested in why he pulled me out into the hallway and interrupted my staring contest with Isla's head.

"I got you into a college for the fall."

What?

"How?"

Headmaster Ellison's eyes brighten, and there's a twinkle there that I've only ever seen a handful of times. "Does it matter? Just make sure you keep doing the work to obtain your actual diploma and you can be off with your friends and my…daughter."

Not all my friends. Some of the group is going in different directions after graduation, but I know Isaiah is following Gemma, and Shiner will be close by too.

The smallest seed of hope plants itself in my chest, but I quickly let it die.

Headmaster Tate grins. "I can tell you're excited, even if your face is remaining the same."

I scowl when the bell rings, and he chuckles. Students start piling out of the classroom door, and although the headmaster is laying out the details of this college I'm supposed to attend, I can't hear him.

My gaze is locked and loaded on Isla and how she pushes her hair behind her ear to show off the soft curve along her neck. My mouth waters, remembering how close my lips were to the delicate skin the other day inside her room. Her pulse thrummed against my fingers, and my dick was harder than I care to admit.

She stops dead in her tracks when she looks past my shoulder. I ashamedly want her to meet my eye, but she doesn't.

"Are you listening to me?" Headmaster Ellison's face pops into my sight, and I shift to lean against the wall.

"Yeah, keep going." I seem engaged, but I'm not.

Isla's sight is set on a woman at the end of the hall, and I can't help but ask the question. "Who is that?" I inch my chin in her direction.

"What?" When he glances at Isla and the woman, his shoulders bundle with a clearing of his throat. "Oh, that's our new school counselor."

"Why is Isla talking to her?"

His arms cross, and he raises an eyebrow. "Oh, are we on a first-name basis with her now?"

If only he knew.

"Pay attention."

"I am," I snap, still keeping my eye on her. "I'm listening."

The headmaster's voice is irksome, but I'm downloading the information he's giving. My gaze remains on Isla, though. She's clutching a book close to her chest and nibbling on her bottom lip. A line of fire races down my spine, and my mouth is dry. Her cheeks turn red, and she's firing off questions to the woman so quickly she can't even answer. Then she turns and storms down the hall, leaving the social worker with defeat written all over her features.

"So, what do you think?"

"About?"

Headmaster Ellison sighs. "Brantley."

"I'm kidding," I lie. "I'll get my diploma. Don't worry."

He snorts, and I'm certain he doesn't believe my feigned excitement, but I'm saved by the social worker when she steps beside me. She glances at Tate, but her gaze is fleeting. That's when I realize she's actually a lot younger than I thought. I decide to keep my questions to myself and slip out between them in search of Isla.

My phone vibrates in my pocket, and it makes me pause. No matter how far away my father is, or the fact that he is currently behind metal bars, the dread is still there. I shake out my shoulders with my phone in my tight grip and sigh at Shiner's name, thankful my mind is only playing tricks on me.

Shiner - Gem just told me that her dad managed to pull some strings and that you're coming to college even though your dumber than a box of rocks and didn't graduate on time.

Me - You're*

Shiner - I used the wrong one on purpose to see if you would correct me. You're smarter than I thought.

I snort.

Shiner - We're going to be the talk of campus
when we introduce those city girls to St.
Mary's famous claiming parties.

Isla's face pops into my head after reading his text, and I stop dead in my tracks. *Get out of my fucking head.* Visuals of her hands against the door with that naughty look in her eye start flying through my mind, and it pisses me off.

I bypass the few students lingering around the hallway and take three steps at a time to make it to my room. My heart is a thundercloud and skipping every other beat. Sweat pelts the back of my neck, and the only thing I can think about is my father's hands on Isla when he finds out that I let her live and how it makes me highly uncomfortable.

He's not going to find out.

My head falls to my closed door, and I exhale all the air in my lungs. I stay holed up in my room way longer than I mean to, and by the time I manage to breathe normally, the sun has set, and the sky is blanketed with stars.

Isla said she's here to find her little brother, but that won't stop me from shoving her out the door and somewhere else. The only thing she will find here is my refusal to help her and a shit-ton of baggage.

The school is quiet and nearly black with the night. I prowl down the hall, stopping at the bend to stare at the girls' hallway. My heart races the more I think about creeping into Isla's room again.

Tell her to leave.

Pack her bags.

Throw her out the goddamn door.

My head turns at a hardly noticeable sound, and I move to the stairway to watch a figure move down the steps in a hurry.

Isla.

I know it's her from the peek of light hair below the hood pulled up on her head. Even with the faint flicker of sconces lining the vast space below, I trail my eyes down her long legs as they stick out from beneath her dress.

I hate that she's wildly hot.

I've been deprived for far too long, and I know she has the ability to quench my thirst like no one ever has before. My body's reaction to her says much more than I care to recognize.

My footsteps follow the ghost of hers, but my eyes are on her shadow. She moves stealthily on the white-and-black checkered floor, and I silently scoff when she doesn't realize she's being followed. I let her get all the way through the front doors of the school before moving to the nearest window to watch. *What is she doing?*

My heart bangs against my crossed arms the more I wait for her next move. I flick my gaze to the two headlights winding up the road and choke with anger when it comes to a stop right in front of her. The moon casts an angelic glow on the side of her cheek, but I note the frown on her face.

The man that exits the car looks old enough to be her father, but I know with full certainty that he isn't. Isla takes a step back. If I were outside, I'd hear the gravel crunch beneath her shoes in her attempt to retreat.

I bite my tongue when she's pulled into the man's chest. He holds her rigid body tightly against his, and I'm choked. A raging dose of protectiveness—or *jealousy?*—forces me toward the door. I inhale the warm summer air but freeze like I'm in the middle of a snowstorm when the car's brake lights dim.

Her icy eyes grip me from the passenger window, but she's gone before I can blink.

An empty pit replaces whatever was filling me, and as

soon as I turn and jog up the stairs, I realize *exactly* what it was.

Or who.

Isla just left with some random man, and I plan to find out exactly who he is to her.

SEVEN

ISLA

My head pounds. I massage my swollen temples with my fingers, opening my mouth a few times to lessen the pain. I'm sick to my stomach and tired down to my bones. I'm tired of playing games and chasing someone who probably doesn't even remember me, but if I stop now, then what?

Heavy feet pull me through the dining hall. The small number of students that are also attending St. Mary's summer school program eye me with suspicion at the lack of food in my hands, but my stomach is tied in too many knots to even consider filling it. I make note that Brantley isn't anywhere to be found, and I still haven't decided if my mind conjured the image of him standing in front of St. Mary's last night when I took off with Zachary or if he really was there.

I'm not prepared to answer questions, so even though it would make me pathetic, I'm hoping it was my mind playing tricks on me in an attempt to be saved from what I was doing in Zachary's presence again.

I put myself in a perilous position by getting in that car. It was risky, and I knew it. Just like I know it isn't a coincidence that Zachary is Thomas's new foster father.

I knew he wouldn't take me to see him, but he did make sure to show me proof with a photo.

"See? He's safe and sound, in the same room you stayed in."

I lean against the wall outside the dining room and bend at the waist so I can see straight. The sting of Raven's news on my brother's actual whereabouts still burns my skin, even a day later—just like Zachary's subtle touches to my thigh inside his car.

"Tired from running off with a boyfriend in the middle of the night, are we?"

I pop up and glare at Brantley from across the expansive hall. He's leaning against the other wall, foot propped behind him in the cockiest stance I've ever seen, with his button-down undone at the top, showing off his hard chest and bouncing Adam's apple.

My eyes are slits, and I deliver a glare like my life depends on it.

The entire reason I'm in this position is because of his father.

"You think you know everything, don't you?" I ask. My chest tightens, and air is hard to come by, so I put my back to him and storm down the hall with fury.

I refuse to let him see me flustered. *Calm down.*

The moment the warm air hits me, it makes me feel even worse. It's thick and sticky, so I run to the closest door I can find and slam it shut.

The floor catches me, and I pull my knees up to rest my forehead on them. I shut my eyes and breathe in and out through my mouth and focus on my surroundings. The smell of chlorine fills my senses, and I think of it instead of every-thing else.

Time passes quickly, and I'm used to the burning scent of

pool water by the time I slowly raise my head. I snap to attention when I realize I'm not alone. *I should have known.*

"You done?" Brantley asks. He's leaning against the doors I rushed through, and it's alarming that I have no recollection of him following me into the…*indoor pool?*

"Done regretting the day I met you? Never." I snap. Pride replaces the anguish in my stomach, and I stand up on shaky legs. "Why are you following me? Are you some stalker or something?"

His throaty laugh echoes around me. *Damn, that's a nice laugh.*

"In case you forgot, I asked you to leave this school. What kind of stalker would do that?"

"You didn't ask." I roll my eyes. "You demanded."

Brantley pushes off the door and creeps closer to me. "And I stand by that. I'll take you anywhere, just as long as you're far away from me."

The nerve.

"I don't understand your hatred for me." I throw my hands up with angry confusion and step backward so I can be farther away from him. "You were the one who hid me in a closet and *saved* me." I use air quotes for more dramatics, but I'm certain Brantley is smart enough to understand my sarcasm. "How dare you act like I did something wrong to you!"

"Maybe I shouldn't have saved you, then." His shoes squeak on the floor as he matches my steps one for one. "I didn't realize you'd be showing up years later to fucking tell me that I owe you."

Anger is a force I'm used to, but standing a mere foot away from a guy who makes me burn hot is something I'm unfamiliar with. I turn, and he does the same. The dark water of the pool is calm behind him, and if I knew how to swim, I'd probably jump in just to put more distance between us.

"You do owe me," I counter. "You and your father are the

whole reason my brother isn't with me. Don't you get it? I'm all he has! You can act haughty and almighty, but you and I both know that we witnessed a murder that night. A murder that wrecked my brother's and my entire fucking lives."

"So you're here to wreck mine? I don't give a shit about you wanting to find your brother, Isla. I'm not helping you, so you might as well leave now before my father realizes who you are." He chuckles, and a hot line of anger pins me to the floor. "For what it's worth, you *owe* me, Ice Princess. I saved you once, and I won't do it again," Brantley snarls. "Oh, and by the way… you're welcome for shoving you in that closet and keeping you calm enough so no one knew you were there. He would have killed you that night if it weren't for me."

Words are nonexistent. I'm angry and resentful, but I'm also indebted to him in a way, and I hate owing someone something.

"I have a great idea."

I move my stare from the pool and meet Brantley's smirk.

"Why don't you get that boyfriend of yours to help you on your righteous quest of finding your brother and get the hell out of my life?"

I'm seething. "He isn't my boyfriend."

The knowing glimmer in his green eyes sends me into overdrive. My hands fly forward, and I shove him as hard as I can into the pool. Water splashes against my bare legs, and a real smile curves onto my face for the first time since entering St. Mary's.

Shit, that felt good.

My smile deepens while I wait for him to emerge with surprise all over his stupidly hot, wet face. A little laugh erupts from my mouth when he pops out of the water like a fish before falling under again.

My smile falls right away, and my heart skips a beat. His hands slap the chaotic waves like he's trying to grab on to something to keep him afloat, and the longer he stays under, the more I panic.

Fuck, fuck, fuck.

Before I know what I'm doing, my shoes are off, and I'm diving headfirst into the water.

Brantley was right.

I do owe him.

EIGHT

The weight of my uniform helps the fake drowning act. I allow the pull of wet cotton to drag me under with a closed-lip smile on my face. It's a dick move, but that's what she gets for shoving me into a pool. Isla wants to act like some violent little brat and feel powerful for pushing me, well she's going to understand the panic that comes with that power.

The air hits my wet face as I spring up out of the water with flailing arms. I catch a quick glimpse of the worry on her face and go back under, hardly holding back my laughter. I pop up again, but she isn't there.

I fling my head to the left and wipe the water from my face. After scanning the area, I finally see her beneath the water. Surprise renders me speechless. *She jumped in after me?* I hover in the water, waiting for her to appear and tell me how much she loathes me, but the longer I float, the more confused I am.

I inhale air, dip under the water, and fight through the burn to see what she's doing. My heart skips a beat when I can't find her. My head emerges, breaking through the waves. *Where is she?*

My eyes sting when I dip back under to search for her. My brain takes a second to catch up to my feet kicking as I dive down to the bottom. A lump of panic pulls me faster when a tangled mess of blonde hair thrashes in front of me. *Fuck.*

I swim fast, ignoring the pang in my chest, and cup her in my arms before pushing off the floor of the pool and shoving us above the surface. She's still coughing when I make it to the side, and I expect her to scramble out of my arms, but she surprises me again. Her shaky arms wrap around my neck, and she holds on tighter. My heart is thrumming like a guitar string, and my body jerks every time she coughs and sputters for air.

The wet strands of her hair get caught in my fingers as I push them out of her face, and I have the sudden urge to put my mouth on hers to give her air. "Are you good?" I clear my throat and look away because my voice came out softer than it should have.

She nods but coughs some more. "I—" Cough. "Thought yo…u—" Cough. "You were drown–" Cough. "Drowning."

I hold her tighter and fling damp hair off my forehead to see her better. "So you jumped in to save me?"

She's quiet, and instead of confirming, she looks away and shows me the glistening side of her flushed cheeks.

"You jumped in to save me from drowning, but you almost drowned in the process?"

Isla's mouth parts like she's going to say something, but she stops herself at the last second. Her entire body trembles in my arms, so I decide to keep her there longer instead of putting her on the side of the pool.

"You can't swim?" She shakes her head. "Why would you jump in if you can't swim?"

Isla shrugs, unwilling to answer.

She obviously doesn't know me, because she *will* answer me.

I press her back against the side of the pool, and she gasps when she realizes I've let go of her. The position forces her to slap her hands against my shoulders, and her legs wrap around my waist next.

Mmm, this is a problem.

I rest one hand against the side of the pool beside her head, and the other grips her wet chin so she can't look away. "Why would you risk your life to save the guy who *ruined* yours?" I ask, using her words against her. "Not many people would save someone they hate as much as you say you hate me."

Isla's soft lips part, and fast breaths shoot out of her mouth and land on mine. *God, why is she so pretty and tempting?* Her blue eyes peer up at me, and I feel the chemistry simmering beneath my skin. I edge closer to her, and her legs clamp onto my hips to keep me in place.

It doesn't work.

My head nestles beside hers, and she turns, giving me access to her neck. I want to sink my teeth into her and suck on the delicate skin to end the madness I feel, but instead, I whisper into her ear, "You're easy to read. You don't hate me at all, do you?"

"I do hate you."

My nose trails her jaw until my lips settle on the corner of her mouth. "You nearly died trying to save me." I press myself into her and dip my hand under the water to pull her closer. *Fuck. Stop.* "And I nearly died saving you years ago. I say that makes us even, don't you?"

Her lips brush mine when she opens her mouth. "Not even…close." She's breathing hard, and I am too.

I can't stop.

I want to kiss her so hard she forgets all about that night, because I want to forget too.

"Will this make us even?" I ask, gripping on to the wet fabric of her plaid skirt, pushing it past her hips. I wait for her to shove me away or tell me no, but her eyes are doe-like, and her white teeth sink into her bottom lip like some little tease. My chest is ready to explode with every labored breath, and I stare long and hard at her reaction when I dip my finger into her panties. Her skin is silky soft, and touching her is an insatiable rush.

Why isn't she stopping me?

Isla's eyes shut, and her head tips backward when I move my thumb over her clit.

"You're not going to stop me?" I probe. There's a big part of me that is slightly afraid that she's going to push me away at the last second. My hand stops moving at the thought. *Shit, she has power over me, and she has no idea.*

"Keep going." Her hips tilt to meet my hand, and I'm a goner. Minutes ago, I wouldn't have done a single thing she asked, and now I'm wading in a pool with her pressed against me, and I'm following her commands like my life depends on it.

"Only if you tell me you'll leave St. Mary's."

Those soul-sucking blue eyes grip me harder than before, and she shakes her head slowly. A whimper escapes when she moves herself just enough for my finger to gently press into her pussy.

I can't fucking breathe.

In an attempt to steal back my control, I pull my hand out of the water and pinch her chin. "Tell me, Isla."

"No."

"Then no orgasm for you." I grin mischievously.

We're playing a game, and I'm on the edge of my seat, wondering what her next move will be.

We are no longer two people who share a traumatic memory together. She's no longer the girl that reminds me of shitty times, and I'm no longer the guy who stood by and watched her father's murder while keeping my hand over her mouth so she wouldn't scream. We're too wrapped up in the moment to remember any of that, and by the timid smile on her face, I think she's having just as much fun as I am.

"I don't need you when it comes to orgasming, Brantley."

She holds on with one hand as the other disappears underneath the surface of the water.

My mouth dries out, and when her head flies backward in pleasure, I *almost* drown.

NINE

I will never be able to get Brantley's face out of my head after seeing the hooded look in his eye as he watches my every move. I have no idea why I can't seem to remove myself from the situation, and I should be angry with how alive I feel in the moment, but that's just the thing.

I feel *alive*.

We're both in a daze–hidden away from the past and all rational thoughts.

"Fuck, you're hot as hell, and I hate it."

I slip a finger further into my wet panties at his compliment and suppress a moan. *Why does this feel so good?* I tell myself it's because I'm in the water and worked up from his hot whispers, but I know it's because I'm teasing him, and he's enjoying it.

My eyes spring open when I feel myself falling underneath the water. When I meet his face, I realize that he's so entranced in what I'm doing, he forgot he was half holding me up in the pool.

He quickly shoves me past the break in the water and slaps me onto the edge of the pool. I'm exposed with him below me, half in the water and half out. His arms rest over the edge, and my legs are spread wide, giving him full access to stare up my wet skirt.

Water cascades over my curves, and my cotton panties are stuck to my body like a second layer of skin. Brantley looks up at me with eyes darker than his soul and then flicks his gaze in between my legs.

"Don't let me stop you from getting what you want, baby."

My voice is breathy even as I try to sound as nonchalant as possible. "Maybe I'm stopping you from getting what you want by not letting you see me touch myself."

He scoffs before pushing his hair off his forehead. I want his strong jaw and mouthy tongue in between my legs, and that makes me feel so dirty but turned on at the same time.

"I want much more than that." His voice is hardly audible. "Even if I keep telling myself I don't."

There's a throb urging me to keep going, and it makes it hard to remember the hate. The anguish that comes with every thought of him and that night slips away, and I forget to breathe altogether when he pushes my knees wider.

I shut my eyes and let myself become fully immersed in the physicality of pleasure. My emotional standing with Brantley is long gone, and I'm feeding off his touch against my skin and his heavy breathing.

There's a soft tap to my inner thigh, and I open my eyes to see Brantley pull back with parted lips. He's concentrating on my face, and I blush. "I hate that you're so damn pretty," he admits.

My cheeks flush deeper, and there's a sense of fulfillment brewing through the hot pleasure. It surprises me enough to miss the fact that his mouth is trailing kisses up my leg.

"It's fucking with my head, Isla."

I swallow and tell myself to get up and leave him in the pool, because how can I let myself be this vulnerable with the guy who holds so much of my trauma in his hands, but his warm whispers of admiration keep me in place.

"Well, seeing you again for the first time since that night fucked with my head," I say.

"Is that why you jumped in to save me?" His breath brushes over my damp panties, and I shiver. I freeze when a gush of air cools my skin and exposes me. If I were to move a fraction, I'd feel the pad of his finger holding my panties to the side. "Can't help but feel something for me because of that night?"

"Hatred," I say, lying straight through my teeth.

Jumping in after him proved that I don't hate him like I say I do. He played a part in my father's death, but I can't help but remember the way he pulled me back into my room multiple times to shield me from the dangerous game my dad was playing. I can tell myself that he ruined my life, but he actually saved it.

"You don't hate me."

I should.

"It feels wrong not to hate you." My heart aches with a truth I'm desperate to ignore, so I start touching myself again so I can feel something other than shame. "You were there, and you left me and my baby brother."

"I know." His voice is strained, so I move my hand faster in an attempt to reach a high so I can forget who we both are. "I was trying to protect you."

"But why?" *I want to know.*

"I wish I fucking knew. I haven't been the same since leaving you in that stupid closet." He makes a frustrated sound before his teeth sink into my thigh, which does nothing but make my blood run hot. My body is twisting, and my stomach hollows. "Your damn blue eyes did something to me that first night I saw you hiding behind the banister to eavesdrop. I can't explain it."

Just like I can't explain *this.*

We are bonded by tragedy, and for some reason, fate has brought us back together.

"That's why I want you gone, Goldilocks. Because I can't get you out of my head." Brantley grips the outside of my thigh, and I let him watch as I bring myself to an orgasm.

"Fuck." I hear his mumble even though my ears are ringing.

Another orgasm peaks when his wet tongue replaces my finger, and I roll my hips to meet his strokes. *Oh my god.* His teeth scrape against my delicate skin, and I grip his hair as we both move as one.

"Fuck me. You taste so fucking good." His praise sends heat to every nook and cranny in my body, and I suck in my cheeks when my high starts to fade.

Shit. Did I really just let him do that?

Our eyes catch, and he's just as surprised. His heavy brow line is furrowed, and the damp ends of his hair are rustled from me gripping it. I quickly slide backward and stand, letting my wet skirt fall to my mid-thigh before backing away slowly with silence following my every move. I slip on my sandals, put my back to him still in the water, and walk out into the courtyard, leaving my dignity in that stupid indoor pool with a guy who is at the center of my worst memory.

I told him he was going to help me find my brother, but after *that*, I'm not so sure I want his help. I'm beginning to think Brantley is just as dangerous as my scheming with Zachary.

At least his mouth sure is.

TEN

I have an obsessive nature.

I'm aware of it—not that it makes it any better.

I know it's a trait I inherited from my father—if his attempts at stalking my biological mother said anything about it. It's exactly why I've steered away from getting too infatuated with someone. Except, now my eyes follow a blonde-haired, blue-eyed ice princess around St. Mary's like she's mine when, in reality, she couldn't be further from it.

Denial is something I'm used to, but tell me why I can't seem to deny myself any part of her that she's unknowingly giving to me. My spit thickens when I look at how short her uniform skirt is, and I suddenly wish I could drag her back into the pool and fuck her instead of letting her touch herself to prove a point.

She's gorgeous and soft in all the right places. She's resilient too, and it's obvious to everyone that she wants to hate me just as much as I want to hate her. It's been four days since I followed her through the courtyard and hid in the natatorium, and I'm becoming more irritable by the hour.

I want her.

Maybe my obsessive nature *started* with her.

Something about that goddamn closet and her head buried in my chest as her father fell to the ground did something to me. Protection flew through my veins, and the only thing I've been able to think about since is how *not* to feel that for anyone else.

But then, Isaiah had to drag me into his bullshit with Gemma, and I found myself risking my life for her.

Then came Journey.

And shortly after, Sloane.

I tell myself that I did it for the guys I consider family, but I'm not so sure that's the truth.

Denial is becoming translucent with Isla involved.

After passing a few guys kicking a soccer ball down the hall, I head to the library and sit down at the farthest computer away from everyone. I can hear my own heartbeat when I bring up the prison database and hit search.

My teeth clank together when I see his name. I sigh with relief, like I do every time I confirm that my father—along with Isaiah's and Cade's—is still locked away behind bars.

It doesn't mean we're safe, but we're safer than before.

Isla's face pops into my head the second I let my guard down, so I exit out of the inmate list and open up another search engine.

I remember her father's name.

I remember his face.

I remember their home address.

I remember looking at the closet door seven hundred times before walking out of the house and leaving her with her wailing brother.

After making sure no one is behind me, I type in her name and wait to see what pops up.

It only takes ten minutes to find her alias–along with her age, race, and a short bio. I rub my hand over my face with unease as I stare at her picture on an adoption website. In the photo, she isn't much older than the last time I saw her four years ago. Her smile is timid, and her blue eyes are bright with fear and a hint of loneliness.

"What are you doing?"

My finger hovers over the mouse, but I don't exit out of the website because there's no use in hiding it now that she's standing behind me. I smooth my expression and turn around to look at her.

"Researching." I raise an eyebrow. "I'd ask what you're doing, but it's pretty damn obvious that you're eavesdropping. Old habits die hard, yeah?"

It's the first time we've spoken since I had my face between her legs, and it's feeding me like I haven't eaten in years. I smirk when she storms over to me, leans down, and exits her biography.

Her neck is right there for the taking, and my stomach twists. I lift my hand and push her hair back further to stare at her beating pulse as she continues to lean into my space.

"That's…none of your business!"

Isla turns her head to me, and our lips *almost* touch before she jumps back and crosses her arms. The pout on her face is adorable. I smirk deeper, and she scoffs.

"You want my help, but I can't know anything about you? That doesn't seem very fair."

My little search has nothing to do with helping her, but she doesn't need to know about my sudden obsession with her.

"I don't want your help anymore." Isla turns and begins walking away, so I stand up and follow after her. I catch up quickly because one stride of mine is three of hers.

"What changed your mind?" I ask, whispering as we walk past the grouchy librarian.

After she doesn't answer me, I wrap my hand around her waist and whisper in her ear, "Afraid you'll spread your legs for me again?"

Fuck, I am toying with her, and I can't stop.

She gapes at me. Disbelief paints her face like it's an empty canvas. "Absolutely not. You aren't going to touch me again. It was…wrong."

But wrong has never felt so fucking right.

"I'm touching you right now."

My heart beats faster, and all I can think about is pushing her up against a wall with her legs wrapped around my waist. *Obsessed.*

Isla puts distance between us after flinging my hand off her waist. Unfortunately for her, it does nothing but make me want her that much more.

"Leave me alone."

I wait for a few other unfortunate summer school students to slink past us before bringing up Isla's problem at hand. "So, you found your brother, then?"

The scowl she's sporting fades, and she glances down the empty hall.

"I take that as a no." I lean against the wall next to the portrait of George Washington and squint at her. "You just don't want my help, then?"

"I don't want *anything* from you."

I chuckle, which seems to make her angry.

"You may not want my help, Goldilocks…" I push off the wall and head toward her. My use of the pet name makes her nose scrunch with disgust. "But you need it."

To my surprise, she doesn't deny it.

"How about this?" I cup her chin and tilt her cute scowl in my direction. I love that I tower over her. "I help you find him, and then I help you find your way out of my life for good."

I'm as tight as a rubber band, and the second she's gone, I

know it's going to snap. I can taste the fear of what comes with pushing her away. I felt something that night in the closet, just like I felt something the moment I saw her name on the whiteboard outside her room. I've felt it ever since, like it's a second skin, which is harrowing to someone like me.

What is she doing to me?

Isla's eyes bounce around the hallway, like she's contemplating my proposal, but then she shakes her head, and my heart skips a beat.

"I don't need your help finding him."

"I thought we've already been through this." My tone is lazy, but I'm twisted on the inside. "You do need my help."

She shakes her head again. "I've found him…" Isla licks her lips before gulping loudly. "I just need to figure out a way to keep him." I follow Isla's swaying skirt down the hall with lingering confusion. Before she disappears, she turns, and the ghost of defeat is haunting her features. "And you can't help me with that."

I wait until she's out of my sight before pulling open my phone and calling an old friend.

Isla has no idea what I can and can't help with, and even though I told her I wanted her out of my life, I know it was a complete fucking lie.

ELEVEN

ISLA

The warm summer breeze whips at the ends of my hair when I tilt my head back to look at the moon. St. Mary's is dark and quiet at my back, and I let myself feel peaceful for a second. The nerves from sneaking through the darkened corridors start to fade, and to my surprise, Brantley is nowhere to be found.

When first arriving at St. Mary's, I thought the headmaster would be a hardass and there would be locks on every door, but I was wrong. Granted, I'm eighteen, and I think most of the students here are, but *still*, we are considered high schoolers to an extent. We're all attending the summer program for a reason. Theirs is probably for a high school diploma; mine is to get closer to my brother. *Tomayto, tomahtoe.*

Two bright headlights shine in my direction, and I slowly rise to my feet. I force a closed-lip smile onto my face. Zachary comes to a sudden stop, and instead of waiting for him to open my door, I do it myself and slide onto the cool leather of the passenger seat.

I can't help but turn around to see if my brother is in the back seat. There is no disappointment when I see that he isn't, because I'm not naive enough to think that Zachary would give me what I want right away.

He wants me to himself, and he knows I'll keep showing up if he continues to taunt Thomas in front of me.

"Did you really think I'd bring him out this late?"

He acts like he's running for foster father of the year.

I whoosh forward in his sports car and stare at the side of his face, noting the five o'clock shadow he's sporting.

"He's at home with Jess. Asleep."

I go straight for the kill because I can't help myself. "And where does your wife think *you* are, Zachary?"

He glances over at me with a raised eyebrow. "Feeling feisty tonight, are we?"

Only because I know that's what he likes.

"She's asleep as well."

Just like the many times he snuck into my bedroom when I lived there.

Vomit hits the back of my throat with regret, and I *hate* him for putting me in the position that he did. But here I am again, allowing him to put me in yet another fucked-up situation.

"Where are we going tonight?" My voice stays neutral with my attempt at staying calm, but on the inside, I'm messy. Chaos fuels my blood, and I'm jittery with thoughts of what tonight will entail.

I don't want this.

But with Thomas being dangled in the background like a toy, I don't have much choice.

Brantley's snarky offering fills my head the longer I'm in the car with Zachary, but there's nothing he can do to help me, even if I *did* want his help.

I've been on my own for years, thanks to his father.

I may have thought I needed Brantley back then, but I most definitely don't need him now.

Zachary puts on his blinker, and I watch in the mirror as St. Mary's gets smaller and smaller. "Somewhere private."

Shit.

"I want something first." The words are out of my mouth before I can stop myself.

I jerk forward with the sudden tap of the brake.

"Oh, is that right?"

His dark eyes level me with suspicion, but he knows me well enough to know I won't back down. "I want to see him."

The roll of his eyes makes me bite the inside of my cheek. "I told you, he's asleep."

"I won't wake him."

"You must think I'm a fool, sweetheart."

For once, the past is on my side. "What makes you think you can't trust me, Zachary? I could have turned on you two years ago." I stare out the windshield and dig my fingers into the leather beside my thighs. "But I didn't. So trust me when I say I won't wake him."

Foster care will teach you that the things you think are unimportant are actually vital to your survival. *Never bite the hand that feeds you.*

Zachary's hands flex against his steering wheel, and I know he's contemplating my request.

"Please, Zachary."

My eyes water with my pleading, but I turn and look out the window so he can't see. Two years ago, I was desperate for attention and love. Zachary used that to his benefit and abused his power as a foster father. He took my vulnerabilities and feasted on them. It took Jess finding out to set me straight and show me that what Zachary was doing was the farthest thing from love. He's a man who likes a thrill, and sneaking into my bedroom while his wife slept two doors down was just that.

My phone call to him after I found out that Thomas was their new foster child—no doubt Zachary's doing—gave him another thrill. I'm not fooled into thinking his subtle touches and sweet nothings in my ear are real. Zachary never cared for me.

It was a sick form of manipulation, just like it is for him to use Thomas to get me back.

And now, he's getting manipulated in return.

"You have to be quick," he says. "If Jess finds you with me, I'm afraid of what she'll do. She has no idea that Thomas is your brother. Different last names and such." He turns and heads for the freeway.

"But you knew, didn't you?" I ask as sweetly as possible, making him think it's a game. My tone is flirty, and it's not hard to hide the glee in my voice because I'm about to see my brother for the first time in years.

"Of course, I knew, sweetheart."

I reach forward and turn up the music to drown out the beating of my heart. I stare out the window at the blurring stars and think of anything but how wrong I feel for being in his passenger seat.

To my surprise, Brantley comes to mind.

He was my safe place once, and admittedly, I haven't felt safe since.

———

My legs shake as I rush up the stairs leading to St. Mary's with my bleeding heart in my hands. Zachary speeds away with his shirt undone and his tie looser than before. I tremble when I grip the iron doorknob, and that's when a tear swells before it falls onto the warm stone beneath my feet. The crickets stop chirping at my quiet sob, and I put my hand up to my mouth to keep myself together.

Thomas is so much older. His once chubby hand was clutching onto the teddy bear I gave him before he was ripped away from me in that same bed I considered mine once before.

WITSEC tried to work with the system to keep us together, and they did a good job at doing so for a couple of years, but after a while, it became difficult. No one wanted a young boy *and* his overprotective teenage sister, so they separated us, and I'm afraid that he doesn't even remember me at this point.

Another slash of hurt gives me whiplash. I almost didn't budge when Zachary pulled me down the hallway away from Thomas, but I knew that I had to play my cards right, so I went willingly.

I was quiet—something I'm used to—even when Zachary pushed me into the bathroom instead of taking me down the steps to *'go somewhere private.'* There is no greater thrill than touching your old foster daughter in the guest bathroom while your wife sleeps down the hall, right?

More tears escape the longer I think about it. I gather the hem of my summer dress, like pulling the cotton down over my thighs is going to take away his touch.

I didn't say no when he trailed his fingers down my spine and pulled me into his chest, and I didn't say no when he nibbled on my ear and put his hand between my legs. *It's just a game, Isla.* My lip wobbles again, and I cry harder, despite my efforts to keep it together. There are so many casualties that come with this messed-up plan, and there's a part of me that wonders if I should just leave it be.

Maybe it would be better if Thomas just forgot about me altogether.

The only problem is that *I* can't forget about *him*, no matter how hard I try. I'm all he has, and he's all I have.

"Shit," I whisper. I wrap my arm around my lower belly to hold myself together. "This is so messed up."

"What is? You sneaking out of the school late at night to go be with your boyfriend?"

I snap my watery gaze in Brantley's direction and drop my arms by my sides from surprise. It only takes me a second to bounce back. "He's not my boyfriend!" Turning away, I wipe my tears and fling them into the dark. "Go away."

"Nah, I enjoy this view."

Me crying? He *would* enjoy it.

I grind my teeth together as moisture spills over my lower lashes. I soften my voice, and I'm damn near about to plead. "Please go." I hate that I'm throwing up a white flag, but my stomach is in knots, and my limbs are still trembling. The energy it takes to argue with Brantley is depleted, and I'm not sure I have it in me to put up a good front.

"If he isn't your boyfriend, then who is he?"

I spin around, forgetting that I'm trying to avoid showing Brantley that I'm upset. "It's none of your business!" My voice rises, but by the end of my sentence, it's more of a croak. I search the dark for him, but it's too late to do anything rash because his hand grips my wrist, and I'm pulled into his chest so hard I lose my breath.

"You're crying"—he wipes a tear and throws it off to the side—"so that makes it my business, Goldilocks."

TWELVE

I do not like the feeling I have from seeing Isla cry. It gives me an itch for violence, which is a thirst I've inherited from years of being next to my father, a thirst I don't want to quench anymore. But watching Isla climb out of that car with tears in her eyes makes me want to burn the expensive vehicle to ash with him still inside of it.

It's some kind of messed up psychological shit that's making me this way, I think. I can't go back in time and stop her father's murder, but maybe if I fix one of her problems now, I can stop obsessing over her.

Guilt. I feel guilty. That's what it is.

"Let me go, Brantley," she demands through a held-back cry.

My chest is tight, and I'm acting irrationally. I reach up and grab the side of her wet face and speak the truth. "I can't." Her salty tears disappear with a swipe of my thumb, and her bottom lip trembles even faster.

She sniffles with a flicker of her jaw. I know she's trying to avoid wearing her heart on her sleeve, but it's so damn beautiful to see the real her. "Why? Enjoying my tears? Loving that I look so weak right now?"

I'm tight all over, and I tell myself to leave her be, but my body refuses to listen to my head. Instead of letting her go, I pull her in closer. "I left you crying once before. I don't plan to do it again. Who is he?"

"No one."

"Don't lie to me."

Isla turns away, but she doesn't take a step backward. Her shoes stay pressed up against mine. "Don't you remember what you told me that night?"

"Unfortunately, I remember everything about that night."

Her eyes are glassy when she turns back to me. "You told me that if I want to live, I'll learn to lie. Now you're wanting the truth?"

I hate that night. "This is different." Her glossy gaze bounces back and forth between mine, and it pulls the truth right out of me. "I told you to lie so you'd stay alive. I wanted you to harden up so you'd have a fucking chance at life." I swallow the rest of that night and move on to the present. "I know why you were crying that night, and I want to know why you're crying right now."

Isla's lips purse as another tear slips down her cheek. "Why do you even care?"

"I don't know." My thumb swipes away another bead of moisture before I grip her quivering chin. "But I do, so either I search that license plate and find out where that man lives so I can burn down his house, or you can tell me why he has you so upset." I try to pretend I'm not jealous, but I fucking am. "Who is he?"

Isla's throat bounces with a soft swallow, and when she looks into my eyes, I swear to God she's looking into my soul. The soft lines around her lips wrinkle with refusal, but she surprises me with the truth. "He's my old foster father."

My heartbeat is in my ears.

"Zachary Welton." It's not a question.

She pulls away, but I drag her in closer. "How do you kn–"

"Why is he showing up here?"

Isla tenses, and a million and one scenarios run through my head. I quickly turn around while keeping a hold of her wrist and pull her toward the school. Once we're inside, we stay silent until we're in my room with the door locked. "What does he have hanging over your head, Isla?"

I know the answer already because it's not hard to put two and two together.

"He either knows where your brother is…" I lean back on my door and pull the hood of my jacket up on my head to seem casual, although I'm anything but. "Or…he *has* your brother."

A soft gasp leaves her. *Bingo.*

Now that we're in my room with more than just the moon as our light, I run my eyes down her body. Thick blonde waves lay over the straps of her summer dress that hits mid-thigh. She looks edible. Pretty but sexy at the same time. I stare at the little space between her legs, remembering what's underneath the fabric, but freeze when I see a mark on her skin. My blood runs cold, and the temperature drops the closer I get to her. The backs of her thighs stay pressed against my bed, but the moment I push her hair behind her shoulder, she tries to escape. My hand snaps out, and I grip her neck lightly, turning her head to stare at the hickey on her skin.

"So, he is your boyfriend?" *Fuck.*

"No!" she shouts, slapping my hand away to scramble out of my grip. I push her down on my bed and trap her there.

"Then explain the mark on your neck, Ice Princess." Shoving her legs apart to show off her panties, I press my thumb onto the other hickey on her thigh. "And the one right here."

Isla quickly gives up. She flops back onto my bed, and I hate that I'm happy she's making my sheets smell like her, especially after she's been touched by another man.

Her hands cover her face. "It's nothing." Her lie is muffled, and it pisses me off.

"Pretty girls never lie," I remind her. "So stop *fucking* lying."

She slowly slides her hands down her tear-streaked face, looking truly vulnerable for the first time since I left her in that closet. I take away the bite of anger in my tone and ask her something I'm not sure I want the answer to. "Did you want him to touch you?"

I let up on her a little, but she's still trapped on top of my bed. Her legs close when I remove my hand from her thigh. I stare at the side of her face when she turns away. "No."

No? My entire body runs hot.

"But it's not what you're thinking."

I remain quiet because I'm not sure what's going to come out of my mouth. The truth is, I don't trust myself around Isla. If the Rebels were here, they'd be giving me so much shit for my behavior. I was always the one Rebel who swore off relationships and all that bullshit, but right now, I can't seem to make sense of what I'm feeling. Anger? Protectiveness Both?

"Then what is it, Isla? Because what I see is a fucked-up man who is taking advantage of you, and I've gotta admit...I don't fucking like it."

Isla turns back to me, and those blue eyes shine with shock. She blinks, and it looks like she's thinking unbelievable things about me, just like I'm thinking about her.

"We had a thing when I was his foster daughter..." She shuts her eyes, like she doesn't want me to see her, and my heart beats harder. "I...I didn't realize how wrong it was. I was lonely and confused and had no one in my corner. They'd taken my brother away from me, and I was broken."

He took advantage of her.

I've known bad men, much worse than Zachary, but it doesn't make him any less bad in my eyes.

"So, he used your vulnerabilities against you and made you feel wanted?"

Isla nods, and I watch as a tear slips out of the corner of her closed eye. *No.*

"His wife found out. She went ballistic. Threatened us both. After things calmed down, she made me promise I wouldn't tell the social worker because she'd never be able to foster another child, and I couldn't take that away from her after everything. The whole reason they became foster parents was because she can't have children." Isla inhaled deeply. "She told me she'd never allow another girl in their house, given her husband's behavior." I stare down at Isla's trembling lip. If I could have choked on my own tongue, I would have. "Now my brother is their newest foster kid, so I guess she stayed true to her word."

"And he did it on purpose, didn't he? To hang Thomas over your head to manipulate you more? He's using Thomas to get you to be in his life again?"

She shrugs timidly. "I was the one that reached out to him when I found out."

She thinks just because *she* contacted him that this is *her* doing? I know a manipulator when I see one. He's probably using Thomas as a reward for letting him fuck her.

I immediately pull away from Isla, and she quickly sits up and stands on shaky legs. She rushes for the door, and even though I swore I'd leave her be to deal with shit on her own, out of nowhere, I reach for her and wrap my palm around her waist. Her back is pressed to my front, and she tenses.

"Wh–what are you doing?" Her question is rushed with panic.

"Stay."

She peers back at me. The small worry lines around her

eyes grow deeper when I raise my eyebrows at her. "I may be an asshole, but I won't use your vulnerabilities against you like that piece of shit. You shouldn't be alone tonight."

Her face softens, and I can't help but think how flawless she is.

I drop my arms and step away from her. I edge my chin toward the bed. "You can have it."

Isla slowly tiptoes past me and sits on the edge without ever taking her eyes off me. I take a knee and slip off her sandals. Chills race up her legs with my gentle touch, and I can say with full certainty that I have never treated someone with such delicacy before.

"I was right," she whispers.

There's a heavy pressure in my chest, and I don't know what to do with it. I'm fumbling on the inside, and I hope she doesn't notice how out of sorts I am.

"What were you right about?" I ask.

Before she answers me, she lies on my bed and turns to her side to curl into a ball. "I was right to feel safe with you."

"I'm not sure how you can say that after everything."

I fucking held her mouth shut while her father was murdered. Sure, I protected her, but how does one come back from that?

Isla shrugs before closing her eyes. "You're good, Brantley. You have been from the start."

My throat closes with emotion, and the longer I stare at her in my bed, the more I realize that I want to believe her assumptions more than anything.

THIRTEEN

ISLA

Wake up, Isla.

I've been telling myself the same thing for years. I can feel myself drifting in and out of sleep and teetering between a dream and a nightmare. Thomas's sweet little hands curled around his teddy bear send warmth throughout, but then it's replaced with a chill and a feeling of hands on me that make me feel guilty, used, and a little dirty.

My eyes open, and I focus on the ceiling above. I inhale deeply before letting the air out, moving my long hair away from my face. I immediately turn to the right and see Brantley's perfect profile. There's a skip in my chest, and I turn away before he wakes to find me staring. I remember everything from last night, and it has left me feeling no less than naked.

Secrets are meant to be kept, and lies are meant to be told. It's a skill I've honed since my father's death, but last night, I told the truth for the first time in a *very* long time, and it left me raw.

Brantley didn't react like I thought he would, and when I felt the bed dip later on during the night, I reached out and grabbed on to him in a half daze.

Skimming my gaze down past my bunched-up dress, I snarl at the hickey on my inner thigh. Shame fills me, and embarrassment lingers closely behind. I pull my dress down hastily and furrow my brows. Brantley doesn't stir when I climb over him. I force myself to take my gaze away from his angled jaw and straight nose. He is peaceful when he's sleeping. No scowl, no darkened gaze as he tries to figure me out. Just *calm.*

I shut his bathroom door quietly and strip out of my dress. Brantley's shower is smaller than mine, but I can't wait another second to wash Zachary's hands from my body. I wait until the bathroom is steamy before stepping onto the wet tiles. The water scalds my skin, and I flinch, but I don't move to turn the temperature down. I scrub the parts of my body that I know are his favorite and try to wash away the fresh memory of his touches.

It wasn't like I told him no, which only makes me feel worse. I'm partly to blame for the way I'm feeling, and that's a bitter truth to swallow.

My heart skips when I hear the bathroom door click open. I freeze with water pelting my back and move my gaze to the tiny slit in the shower curtain. All I can see is Brantley's bare feet beside my bundled-up dress. I want to say something snarky, but it's almost as if he's holding my tongue hostage.

I press my back against the tile when I see his long finger hook on the shower curtain to make the gap larger. I tilt my chin with my arms down by my side when our eyes meet. He's waiting for me to tell him to go. His eyebrow lifts with a challenge, and I surprise us both when I lift mine right back. A hot thrill starts at the top of my head and flows right in between my legs when he skims his heated gaze down my body.

It feels like years have passed before he opens the curtain farther. A hot swallow works its way down my throat, and I can't seem to catch my breath. Water is pelting the side of my body, and the little beads of moisture traveling in between my breasts feel like a tease.

Brantley narrows his eyes, and I swear the green electrifies when he steps into the shower. He's fully clothed, and I want to ask what he's doing, but I can't fathom speaking. I gasp with pleasure when his palms fall to my waist, and he pulls me into his chest. I peer at him through wet lashes as he stares down at me like he wants to say something, but I don't give him the chance.

I rise to my tiptoes and press my mouth against his.

I'm left completely breathless when he kisses me back.

There's a connection so deep I forget where I am.

Brantley's tongue lashes out against mine, and another gasp leaves me when he presses us both against the wall.

I shove at his soaked shirt, and he pulls it off before taking my mouth again. The kiss is fast and swift, but that's how it always is with us. Everything we say and do has been backed with an urgency since the very beginning.

"Do you know how long I've wanted to kiss you?" Brantley's hand trails to the front of my body, and I breathe raggedly in anticipation with a shake of my head. "Longer than I care to admit to myself."

I bite my lower lip and stare at him. He takes it as an invitation and trails his finger down the rest of my body before it hovers between my legs.

"I came in here to ask if you were okay."

I swallow and spread my legs with the tap of his finger.

"But now I'm here to ask if you want me as badly as I want you."

I do.

His finger swipes over my clit, and a soft whimper gives away all my cards.

Brantley has one hand in between my legs, and the other cradles my face with force. Water droplets fall off the edge of his nose and onto his lips when he speaks. "Tell me you want this, Isla."

I peer up at him. "I only want it because it's you…" I catch my breath and lick the water off my lips. "And not him."

Brantley mumbles under his breath. "Good girl."

FOURTEEN

BRANTLEY

One kiss.

That's all it took.

I touch her like I know what love is, and the more I skim my palms over her curves and suck on her delicate skin, the more I crave.

"I'm becoming obsessed with you, Isla." I grip her face to hold her steady. Her doe-like eyes widen, but there isn't an ounce of fear in them. I flare my nostrils and wish I could stop myself from touching her, but I can't. "Stop looking at me like you want me to be obsessed with you."

She swallows before hitching a slippery leg around my waist. I'm in nothing but my soaked boxers, and the only thing on my mind is *her*. My stomach hollows out, and my movements are jerky. I'm not nervous. Instead, I'm fucking *exhilarated*.

My palm splays on the side of her thigh, and her breasts push against my chest. *Fuck.*

I ravage her mouth and strip my boxers off at the same

time. A hot moan leaves her, and it goes right to my dick. I've never been so infatuated with fucking someone, and I've never heard a more perfect sound than her subtle whimpers.

"God," she breathes out.

The pleasure chokes my dick, and I grip her tightly to hold her steady. She grabs onto my wrist and stares into my eyes. Her blue eyes are dazed, and when I slide into her, they close altogether. "Don't stop." Her breathy words are dangerous.

"This is fucking…" I can't speak. Her tight little cunt clenches me, and it's already the best sex I've ever had. My fingers dig into her soft flesh, and I kiss her long and hard. I'm eating up her orgasm and practically choking on her hot tongue. Her legs fall swiftly to the wet tile when I pull myself out of her and grip my dick. Ropes of cum blend in with the water against her belly, and I'm still gripping myself when she peers up at me through her thick eyelashes. I slap my hands against the wall beside her head, and we watch as my cum slips down her stomach and onto the wet floor.

My thumb rubs over her swollen bottom lip like it has a mind of its own, and even though it feels too intimate to speak, I still have the ability to say something that stuns us both. "Remember when I said I'm becoming obsessed with you?"

She nods.

"That just sealed the deal."

Isla looks away like she's just as perplexed as I am. Her voice is low and muffled from the shower. "I think you're just obsessed with protecting me. Making up for what happened in the past."

I grab onto her wrist when she reaches for my shampoo. Her chin lifts, but she doesn't meet my eye.

"Look at me," I demand.

She sighs but does as I say.

"I am obsessed with protecting you."

Her chin quivers but only for a second.

"But I'm obsessed with watching you too. And thinking about you. And being in the same room as you." Confusion masks her fear, and I push her hand down by her side so I can grab the shampoo instead. I have no idea what I'm doing. It just feels *right* for the first time in my life instead of forced. "I'm obsessed with touching you, and I think I'm about to become obsessed with taking care of you too." I squirt some shampoo onto my hand.

"Brantley."

"Just accept it, Isla. Because the way I see it…" My hands are in her hair, and she sighs wistfully. "I'm not giving you a choice."

———

Isla's blonde hair covers half her face, and I itch to move the strands away so I can see her better, but I need her asleep, so I keep still.

My phone is on my chest, and it vibrates with an incoming text from the group chat I started.

Gemma- If your "friend" were to want custody of a sibling because of extreme circumstances, like no other family members, etc., they could apply. But there are stipulations they have to follow–a stable home, a job, those types of things. They would have to show the court that they are capable of providing for their younger sibling.

Isaiah- What friend?

I click out of the group with Isaiah and Gemma and start a new one with only Isaiah and Cade. I repeatedly told them how foolish they were to care for someone after knowing the lengths our fathers will go to in order to ruin our lives, but from where I'm sitting, with a fucking angel sleeping beside me, I think I'm beginning to understand.

I'm not going to pretend like I know what love is, but whatever I'm feeling is strong enough to persuade me that my future doesn't have to look so bleak, and that some things are worth the risk. Like her.

Me- I get it now.

Cade- Get what?

It takes Isaiah a few minutes to respond, but when he does, he's right.

Isaiah- He understands what it feels like to care for someone.

I turn my screen off and slowly crawl out of bed. Isla stirs for a second, but when she turns to her side, she pulls the blanket up higher on her face and falls back into her slumber.

I peer out the window and see a small-framed body leaving the school, walking up to the headmaster's house. I caught on to our newest counselor's field trips shortly after I started to follow Isla. The only difference tonight is that Isla is staying put instead of sneaking away like her old social worker.

I lean against the window and wait.

She'll be back, but instead of rushing to her room in the other wing of this school, she'll be pleasantly surprised when she sees me waiting for her, and even more when I tell her what she's going to do for Isla.

Or for me.

FIFTEEN

There's a faint touch against my skin that feels good but tickles at the same time.

A chill breaks out along my flesh, and my eyelashes flutter before my eyes, and I realize I'm in Brantley's room. His warm mouth presses against my neck, and it doesn't take long for my breathing to accelerate.

"Spread your legs," he whispers in my ear before biting down on my lobe and giving it a little tug.

His mouth is so hot, and I do as he says. I have no idea how we found ourselves tangled up in one another like this again, but I think we're both too caught up in each other to put a stop to it.

"What if I say no?" I tease with a sleepy voice.

A tiny smile curves onto my face when Brantley pauses and looks down at me. His fingers grip my shirt, and the fabric is taut with tension. His hair is messy in an adorably hot way, and when his tongue jolts out to lick his lips, I have zero regrets about showing up at his door *again*.

"I dare you." Brantley raises an eyebrow, and I laugh.

The tight hold on my T-shirt loosens, and my smile fades.

"Do that again," he urges, looking at me like he's seen a ghost.

"Do what?" I hesitate.

"This." Brantley pokes my side, and I squeal. I try to scramble off his bed, but he climbs on top of me and does it again and again until I'm full-on laughing through choppy breaths.

"Brantley! What are you doing?" I laugh again when I try slapping his hands away.

I'm out of breath by the time he stops, and his smile is so genuine it hurts my chest.

"I could get used to that." Brantley is suddenly serious again.

"Get used to what?" My legs open when Brantley's hips tilt toward mine. Our laughter is gone, and his tickles are replaced with subtle, lustful touches.

"Hearing you laugh in my bed." His fingers are in my panties, and it takes less than a minute to get me so worked up I'm panting. I shut my eyes, and my head falls back when he enters me, and it's just as breathtaking as the other times he's touched me.

It's like he can't get enough of me, but I can't get enough of him either. Time is nonexistent when I'm with him. It's only been a few days since he caught me coming back to the school after seeing Zachary, but it feels like I've known him all my life. With Brantley, there's so much *more* involved. We have some insane connection, and maybe it's from that night so long ago, when he risked his life to save mine, or maybe it's just fate, but whatever it is, I'm terrified it's going to be ripped away from me.

"Look at me." My eyes open, and I stare into Brantley's as he works my body to the brink. Sweat forms on his hairline and falls to my body. "That's it, baby," he encourages.

My body reacts to his words, and the confidence flows off him effortlessly. "You like when I call you baby?"

Heat rushes to my cheeks, and he shakes his head while picking up the pace. "Don't shy away. It's just me."

"I barely know you." I gasp when his thumb grazes my clit.

"You know me better than anyone," he admits. "Trust me."

My eyes shut when I orgasm quickly. Brantley curses under his breath when he pulls out of me, but before he can spill onto my stomach, I hurriedly sit up and grip him.

"Wh–"

I shove his hand off his dick and replace it with my mouth.

"Fuck." Brantley's hand grabs the back of my head, and he thrusts twice into my mouth, hitting the back of my throat. I wince, but then he's coming, and I'm swallowing quickly as he thrusts his hips.

As soon as he's done, I slowly pull him out of my mouth. He's staring down at me with a look so heated I'm unable to do anything except take the back of my hand and wipe it over my mouth.

"Jesus Christ," he mumbles. "I've never seen a hotter fucking image in my life."

I smile timidly when he grabs my chin and rubs his thumb against my bottom lip before picking me up and taking us both to the shower.

———

The bell rings, and I rush out of the classroom in hopes that Brantley won't follow me, though I know he will. His presence is heavy, and his shadow falls in line with me right away.

"You gonna tell me what's wrong? Or do I have to force it out of you?" He takes my books from my hands and adds them to his pile.

Being alone with Brantley inside his room with the truth hidden is one thing. But being in a semi-crowded hallway with too many eyes and ears is another. The chaos hit me the moment I was alone. Zachary is still dangling my brother around in the background, and I'm not sure what to do about it other than play the game I started as soon as I found out his ploy. Brantley's warning about his father wanting to kill me lingers on the edge of my worries too. It does nothing but add to the disarray in my head.

I peer at Brantley through clear eyes and sigh. I pull us under a small stone archway until we're blanketed in darkness and wait until the footsteps from students slowly disappear before opening my mouth. Only, Brantley beats me to the punch.

"Isla, fuck." He grabs my hand and places it on his chest. His heartbeat rams against my palm, and my lips part. "I don't know what the hell I'm doing."

"What do you mean?"

"I mean, *this*. Us." Brantley's groan echoes around us. "I don't like feeling like this. I don't like that my heart is beating out of my fucking chest with the thought of something being wrong with you."

Emotions clog my throat, and it takes me a second to breathe. "I…" I clear my throat and look away, even though he can't see me in the dark. "I don't know what I'm doing either." A sigh escapes us both, but I'm the first to break the tension. "I'm just doing what feels right, even if part of me thinks it might be wrong."

He gulps, but I keep spilling things that I haven't even fully processed yet.

"If I think too much about everything, it gets too messy."

Brantley finds my waist and drags me closer to him. "Everything feels right when I'm with you."

My stomach fills with butterflies, and I'm rendered speechless. How can so few words make me feel something indescribable? I press my cheek into his hand when he cups my face. "Tell me what's wrong, Isla. I can tell something is wrong with you."

"How can you tell?"

I am damn good at hiding my emotions. It's astounding that he knows something is up with me.

"I just can." A sarcastic huff falls from his lips. "I don't understand it, so don't make me explain."

A little smile curves onto my face, but it's gone a second later when I'm forced to swallow my pride. "Zachary called."

The strands of my hair tighten in his grip. "What did he say to you?"

Tension fills the small area, and my guard fly up so quickly it's like they never came down to begin with. "He wants to see me tonight."

Silence follows, and I suddenly feel *lost*. I don't know what I'm supposed to do.

"Brant–"

"Okay."

I glance around the dark alcove with utter surprise. My walls slowly start to come back down, and my shoulders relax with his response. "I thought you'd be angry."

"How can I be angry when the only reason you're not with your brother is because my father murdered yours?" Brantley's words are clipped, and the air around us becomes heated. "And I could have stopped it."

"You were a kid, Brantley."

It's the first time I've ever admitted aloud that I don't necessarily fault him for that night.

"So were you."

Silence cages us, and we stay trapped inside the small, musty area for too long. Brantley finally grabs on to my hand and drags us back into the hall. He doesn't let go of my hand until we're safely tucked behind his closed door and on top of his bed.

SIXTEEN

BRANTLEY

"I cannot believe she didn't tell me." Raven, the woman the headmaster is secretly fucking even though she's half his age, whispers from beside me.

My mouth stays shut because my head is too messy to form rational thoughts. Going behind Isla's back is an act she'll see as betrayal, but I know it's the right thing to do, even if she'll hate me afterward.

It's probably better that she does hate me, because then I'll be forced to let her go. Rationally, it's a good move because how can there ever be a future for us when we share a secret that's not only gruesome but also traumatic? Our pasts are interlinked with so much suffering that I'm just waiting for the moment she realizes who I really am. Not to mention, my father is still a threat to us both.

"I also can't believe you blackmailed me into doing this *your* way."

I snort before glancing at Raven. We're both crouched on the ground, waiting for Isla to sneak away into Zachary's car.

My stomach is in knots, but Isla told me to do what feels right, and even though my head is telling me that this isn't the right thing to do, I know in my bones that it is. My thoughts are fueled by my father's gruff voice telling me to kill the bastard and dispose of his body the same way he did Isla's father, but I made the decision to back Isaiah and force our fathers into prison–which means ending all unlawful acts. Otherwise, I'll end up just like him, and that's never fucking happening.

My knees come up and act as ledges for my arms. "I can assure you that you do not want me to do this another way."

Months ago, I would have gathered the Rebels and put this man in the ground. Permanently.

Raven sighs. "I should have pulled her aside and told her what I was planning to do with Thomas."

I shake my head. "She would have never agreed to it, and you know it. Not to mention, you technically have no authority over her. Or Thomas. Especially not with your new position here." I put my attention back on the front doors of St. Mary's. My heart is pumping harder than usual, and adrenaline tingles the tips of my fingers.

"You know her pretty well for only meeting her for the first time a few weeks ago."

I snort again. St. Mary's newest guidance counselor isn't going to get shit out of me, even with the tick of curiosity coming from her.

"And you know Tate pretty well for only meeting him for the first time a few weeks ago," I counter, eyeing her for a quick second to see her cheeks ripen with heat.

"That's none of your business."

I shrug. "Lucky for you, I keep my business to myself as long as everything goes to plan."

Raven sighs again, and we sit in silence for another half hour before I start to get overly antsy. I jump to my feet, and she does the same. "What are you doing?"

"He should have been here by now."

"Maybe she knows that Thomas is going to be with a new foster family."

I shake my head and start for the doors. "He wouldn't risk telling her, because that's the only thing tying them together." Manipulative men are smart.

"Well then, where is he?" Raven looks around and nibbles on her bottom lip.

"Raven?"

We both turn at the sound of the headmaster's voice. *Great.*

"Tate." Raven's voice brims with guilt, and she turns to look at me at the exact same time the headmaster does.

He puts his hands on his hips and sighs disapprovingly. "Go on and tell me, Brantley. I've known you far too long to deal with the bullshit, so what's going on with Isla?"

My eyebrows crowd before I chuckle. "Gemma called you, didn't she?" *Damn her.*

"Sucks to have a friend whose father is the headmaster, huh?"

He looks so pleased with himself as we all shuffle into his office. Raven fills the headmaster in about Zachary and how he's using Isla's younger brother as leverage to get to Isla.

Tate groans with a rub of his face. "Go get Isla."

I teeter between telling him to fuck off, but instead, I turn to head to Isla's room. I told her I had no idea what I was doing when it came to her, and that much is obvious by the pounding of my heart backing every one of my movements.

I'm not even in the hallway yet when the door to the school opens. I spin and see her standing there with her hands down by her sides.

"What did you do?" Isla punctuates every word with force.

I get right to the point because there is no need to mince

my explanation. *Fuck, she knows.* "What needed to be done. I'm not going to let some asshole manipulate you."

Isla's gasp is nothing more than a warm breath, but it slaps me all the same.

"Isla." Raven pops out of the headmaster's office, and Isla's jaw drops open before she sends a scorned look in my direction.

The tiny sliver through the door lets in *just* enough sound that I hear her getaway car idling behind her. My pulse strums, and I crack my knuckles.

"Don't you *dare* come closer to me." There's a hint of panic masking Isla's feeling of betrayal. "I never should have trusted you. *God.*" The heels of her palms go into her eyes, but when I take a step closer to her, she pulls them away and shoots me a glare. "You've ruined everything. *Again.*"

"That's not fair." I stay calm, but my gut is heavy with dread. "I saved your life that night, Isla."

"And you ruined it too!"

I shrug. "Fine. Hate me. Don't trust me. But have enough fucking decency to accept help when it's standing right in front of you. I couldn't help you after that night, but I'm here now. *Helping* you."

Raven tries to ease the conversation because she sees the small steps Isla is taking backward. "Zachary is using Thomas to get to you."

"You think I don't know that?" Isla laughs, but it's not the same laugh I heard earlier when she was wrapped in my arms.

"This is why I came to you." I'm speaking to Raven, but I refuse to take my gaze from Isla. "Nothing is going to stop Isla from seeing her brother."

Isla quickly turns her back to us, and my world stops spinning. Panic like I've never felt cements my feet to the floor as I watch her descend the stone steps of St. Mary's and get into the car of a man who has no idea what kind of girl he has in his passenger seat.

"Isla!" Raven runs after her, but I remain in the same spot. "Do not get in that car. Thomas is being placed in a different home."

Isla is halfway in the passenger seat when I hear Zachary's voice. "You sure about that?"

Raven makes her down the stairs and I follow after her. I take one step at a time and stare at Isla the whole time. "Isla." Her name rolling off my tongue sounds like a prayer.

Her blue eyes harden with an independence that only someone like her can yield. "I'll admit that I needed your help four years ago, Brantley. But I don't need it now."

Yes, you do.

"Get in the car, Isla."

"I will have you arrested!" Raven shouts.

The headmaster's voice is a whisper behind me. "She's eighteen, Raven. Technically, he's doing nothing wrong, and she can make her own decisions. We can't have him arrested."

I want to crack Zachary's windshield with my fist. I want to pull him out of the driver's seat and do to him what I wanted to do to my father on so many occasions. I want to take my fist and plummet it in his face just like my father used to do to me whenever I showed any decency to someone other than him, but instead, I reach down into the passenger seat and grip Isla by the chin with so much force the pads of my fingers turn white.

"I hate you." Isla peers up at me with glossy eyes.

"You can hate me. I'll take it. But listen to what I'm about to say to you because I'm only going to say it once. Do with it what you may." It takes everything in my body not to reach past her and take her old foster father's head and slam it into the steering wheel. "Get out of the fucking car and take the help I should have given you four years ago, because I won't offer it again."

A second passes, but it feels like a year. "No."

And there goes my restraint.

I snap my attention to Zachary, and he smiles before shifting it into drive and pushing the pedal to the floor. I'm forced to let go of Isla's chin so I don't drag her out of the car and cause us both to be run over.

The headlights fade in the distance with Raven still arguing with the headmaster in the distance. That same feeling of dread and emptiness I felt four years ago after I left Isla and her baby brother screaming in a big, fancy house weighs on me the longer I stand outside of St. Mary's.

I walk past Raven and the headmaster, headed for my room. A numbness has started to spread throughout my entire body, and the only person that has ever been able to pull me out of it is the one who just put it there.

SEVENTEEN

ISLA

"What the hell was that all about?"

Nausea grips my stomach, and I can't tell if it's because of Zachary's erratic driving or if it's because of Brantley's departing words to me.

"Is it true?" I grip the door handle. I know I can't open the door and make it out without serious injury, but it grounds me for a moment. "Is Thomas being placed with a different family?"

I hate how they toss foster kids around like they're a sack of potatoes. He needs stability.

"No. You've seen him with your own eyes, Isla. He's comfortably sleeping in his bed, and that is where he'll stay."

"I want to talk to him."

Zachary slaps the steering wheel, and I jump. "Isla, I can't do that. He will tell Jess."

I'm on edge, and he can tell. "You've found a way to hide things from her before. Find a way to hide this."

"Or what, sweetheart? Gonna go back to that boy who

would fumble in the dark with your body if ever given the chance?"

I almost laugh, but the thought of Brantley takes the sting of amusement away almost instantly. I press back into the leather seat and level my voice. "Or I'll tell Jess you've been fucking me again behind her back."

He taps the brakes, but I expect it, so I don't jerk forward. I turn toward him. "Take me to see my brother right now!"

He shakes his head, but he knows I've got him in a choke-hold. The drive takes less time than it should, and when we pull up to the house, he turns the engine off and stares at me long and hard. "I know that you know I orchestrated Thomas being in our care so I could have an excuse to see you again."

I nod.

"I'm sure you see me as nothing but a manipulator who has an unhealthy infatuation with you."

I swallow. Zachary leans forward and places his hand on my thigh. "You've never told me no when I've gone to touch you, though." *I want to.* "Which makes you just as much of a manipulator as me, sweetheart."

My teeth clank together, and I flare my nostrils with unshed emotions. *He's right.*

"Stay here. I'll get Thomas."

Something bright sparks in my belly, and he laughs lightly. "Didn't think I'd actually do it, did you?" His lip tips. "You can thank me after."

I exhale out my held breath when he softly shuts his car door and heads through the garage. The house I thought was a home disappears when I close my eyes, but the only thing I see behind my eyelids are Brantley's green eyes.

"Fuck." I pull on the ends of my hair and stare at the garage door, waiting to see Zachary holding my little brother in his arms. After several minutes pass and no one comes, I start to feel panicky.

Zachary's phone is in the center console, so I pick it up

and enter his password, remembering it from a year prior when I lived with him. I keep the screen on for light as I open the door and step onto the cobblestone driveway.

My toes tingle with anticipation, and I tread softly through the garage to the door that leads into the expansive kitchen. The house is entirely too quiet for my liking.

I stare at the stairs that lead to the bedrooms and listen intently for movement. It isn't until I'm halfway up the steps that I hear Jess. "Tell me now, or I swear to God, I will shoot."

"Wh…what's going on?"

I choke on a gasp and rush up the stairs, straight to the little voice that I know belongs to my brother. He's in my arms before he stumbles down the hallway in his sleepy state, and my first reaction is to put him in the closet to hide, but a grip on my hair has me flying backward.

I scream, and the phone goes flying forward into Thomas's room as I fiddle with the buttons on the screen, praying they call someone. *Anyone.*

"Are you kidding me? You again?" Jess is near hysterics, and the fear on Thomas's face sends instant tears to my eyes.

"*Closet,*" I mouth to Thomas.

He runs, and the slightest feeling of relief hits me.

If he has to watch me die, he'll turn out just like me.

Alone and untrusting of anyone who is willing to help.

Brantley. I should have let him help me.

"Jess. Calm down. You don't understand!"

I'm jerked harder, and I shout from pain. Zachary is in my peripheral, and so is a black gun. My heart is in my throat, and I close my eyes because I can see the outcome before it happens.

"You're fucking her again! What don't I understand?"

The shuffling stops, so I open my eyes to see Zachary take a step back. He's facing both of us now. "Jess, put the gun down. You're acting insane. Look at you!" Zachary throws his hands up and points to me. "You're pulling a girl by her hair down the hallway while pointing a gun at me."

"You made me this way." Zachary rolls his eyes but springs into action when she pulls on my hair again. "And she did too."

He's in front of me one second, and the next, he's not.

All the oxygen in the hallway leaves as his body slams into the floor below my feet. My mouth opens, but nothing comes out. There's a ringing in my ears that takes me back to a dark closet with someone's arms around me, and that's where my mind makes me stay, even as I feel something press against my temple.

EIGHTEEN

BRANTLEY

I lean against the window inside her room and stare at the black lines that Zachary's tires made when he sped away from St. Mary's. My blood isn't pumping with anger, and my heart isn't speeding through my chest. Instead, there's a hole that seems to grow bigger the longer she's with him.

I told her I wouldn't offer my help again, but it was a lie. Years could pass, and if she were to show up and ask for my help, I'd give it.

The window fogs with my sigh, and I storm toward the door, ready to burn her room to ash. I pull on the handle but stop abruptly when I hear something near her bed. I find the device right away. The phone is ancient and looks like it's been dropped a time or two over the years with little indents and scratches on the sides.

"Hello?" A hopeful thought slips in past my denial that it'll be Isla, but instead, there's nothing but a muffling on the other end.

I pull the phone away from my ear and see that the call is still connected.

"Is someone there?" I listen intently. Just when I start to grow pissed at myself for hoping it was Isla, I freeze when I hear a timid child's voice.

"Hel...hello?"

My brows fold. "I'm here. Who is thi–"

Oh fuck.

"Thomas?"

"I need help."

Every muscle locks.

"Something bad happened."

Isla.

"Hide." I don't even recognize my voice.

"I ran and hid in the closet." For someone as unemotional as I am, I feel unhinged at the sound of his fear.

"Tell me what happened, but stay quiet."

I'm almost to Tate's office when Raven catches me in the hall. I put the phone on speaker and mouth, *"Car. Now."*

Raven pulls me behind her, and we're halfway to her car when we hear a loud pop through the phone. My world stops but only for a split second. "Call 911," I say to Raven. "7678 East Elm Street."

"Thomas? Are you okay?"

Raven curses under her breath while dialing 911. We're already rushing from St. Mary's when Thomas whispers through the phone, "I hear yelling, and it's getting closer." He whimpers, and I know the fear he's feeling. I felt it so many times before, at an even younger age than him.

Raven talks toward the phone. "The police are on the way, Thomas."

There is more shuffling on the end of the phone, and when I hear Isla's frantic voice, my entire body comes alive. "Thomas, run! Now!"

"Isla!" I shout, putting the phone up to my mouth.

"Brantley?" She's out of breath, and her words fumble through the phone so quickly I barely catch them. "I'm sorry. It wasn't your fault, and I don't hate you. Take care of him for me ple–"

There's a loud noise, like the phone was dropped on a hard floor, and then the call ends.

"Hurry," Raven says into her phone. "There's a small child and his older sister in danger. I can confirm there is a gun on the premises, and I believe someone was shot."

I put my head in between my knees and breathe in and out of my nose like I used to do whenever I had to accompany my father on his *jobs*. The only difference is that, this time, I'm on the other end of it.

———

I'm out of the car before Raven comes to a stop. The street is painted with hues of red and blue, and there's caution tape holding back random bystanders. Everything moves in slow motion, and I scan the chaos for her pretty blue eyes, praying to whoever will listen that she's still alive.

There is no use in thinking about the what-ifs and hating myself for not pulling her out of that fucking car, but I can't stop myself from spiraling anyway. I'm standing in the middle of the road with my heart in my hands, and the only thing I can hear is my heartbeat. I run my gaze around the chaos, and that's when something catches my eye. I stare at the hidden shadow before prowling toward it. The farther away I get from the house and bystanders, the more anxious I become.

The shadow moves, and nausea grips me. I know who it is before I even lay eyes on him.

Thomas is hiding behind a parked car, and when our eyes meet, shock ripples the ground around me. He looks just like his older sister.

I continue to walk toward him and subconsciously put my hands up in caution. The red and blue lights from the police cruisers flicker across his cherub-looking face.

Round cheeks, hair as white as snow, and eyes so blue and full of fear. I do something that is completely out of the ordinary. I reach out and scoop him up into my arms and lower my voice. "It's okay. I've got you, Thomas."

I do what should have been done for me when I was his age. There were so many times I wished someone would show up to take me away and tell me that everything was going to be okay.

It never happened, though.

But I'm here now, and Thomas and Isla are both going to get what they deserved four years prior—someone to come swoop them up and take them away from the bullshit.

Thomas is tense at first, but then he buries his head into my shoulder and holds on tight. I stand in the middle of the road, and although everyone seems to be staring at me, none of them are Isla.

Where the hell is she?

I spin and scan the crowd. It's silent in my head, and I know if I let myself hear, it'll be a distraction, so I keep the distractions to a minimum, hold on to Isla's brother tightly, and stare at the house with the numbers 7678 on the front.

Thomas's hands dig into my neck when I start toward the house. My stomach churns, and my body goes numb. I think back to four years ago when I hid her in that closet. It was the first time I'd ever done something like that behind my father's back. Isla was my own little gateway drug, and all it took was one look in her direction again to pull me right back through.

She means more to me than she knows.

Thomas shifts in my arms. "Isla."

I spin around and stagger at the sight of her.

Isla is surrounded by police officers, and my heart skips a

beat when our eyes meet. Her long blonde hair flows over her shoulders and sways with her steady steps. The silver blanket wrapped around her shoulders falls off with the summer breeze, and her blue eyes catch the light from the moon. I almost fall to my knees.

I walk Thomas over to meet her halfway. There is nothing I can say that will express the relief I feel, so I pull her in close, and we stand together with her little brother in between us. He's still gripping my neck, like I'm the only safe place he's ever known, and his sister is doing the same.

"We need you to come sit down and get checked out." I glare at the EMT, and they remain in the same spot, unfazed by my glower.

"Tell me you're okay." I move to see her better, but Thomas grips me harder, like he's afraid I'm going to let go of him.

"You came." Isla blinks away tears in her eyes.

I'm still holding on to her brother, but I take one hand and grab her chin, tilting it toward me. "I'll always come when you need me—even when you say you don't."

Her head hits my chest, and her shoulders shake. I feel her cry harder when Thomas reaches one of his arms around her head to hold her in place. My lips touch the top of her head, and I kiss her there. It's a sweet gesture and one I've never done before, but it feels right, just like it always has with her.

EPILOGUE

A nervous breath wobbles out of my mouth as I sit in the chair at the foot of the headmaster's desk. Raven is biting her nail as she rests on the end of the mahogany.

"What are your thoughts?"

I move my attention to the headmaster before glancing back at Raven. She is on the edge of her seat–no pun intended.

My fingers dig into the arms of the chair, and I try to pull in my emotions. I bet I look so vulnerable to them, sitting here in this chair, trying to make a decision about my four-year-old brother's future because I'm the only thing he has.

"There are some things you don't know," I start. "There are some things *he* doesn't know."

Like how Brantley's father murdered mine, and that's why I was in WITSEC, or like how Brantley's father would probably kill me if given the chance.

"Isla." I glance at the headmaster as he rises from his chair and rounds his desk. He leans against it, right beside Raven. "There are things you don't know as well."

"Like?" I ask.

Raven puts her hand on his for a brief second before pulling away. "Like where I grew up before I attended St. Mary's and how I'm privy to the lifestyle your father led before he was murdered." I try hard not to look surprised. "I'm an orphan too. Why do you think I've taken such an interest in you?"

I shrug, but for once, it's not out of spite. It's actually because I was unaware.

The headmaster clears his throat. "Let's just say that we're both acquainted with how some secrets just need to stay buried."

My tongue pushes into my cheek before I sigh. "Are you sure you don't want to know?"

"We're sure."

I roll my lips together and give in. "Okay, then I guess I'm on board."

I'm swimming in relief. Thomas will be under the care of Raven and live on the grounds of St. Mary's. I'll finish the summer program and obtain my high school diploma before deciding what the future looks like without the thought of having to make ends meet for a little boy who deserves much more than I will ever be able to give him.

The headmaster and Raven stand at the same time. I meet her soft gaze when she kneels down below me and puts her hands on my knees. "Bribery always works."

I laugh softly and jokingly roll my eyes before standing up and leaving them to discuss the logistics of living arrangements and Raven's continued employment at St. Mary's.

Thomas is safe and sound at the headmaster's house, no more than a football-field-length away from me, and for the first time in four years, I feel like I can relax.

St. Mary's is a web of confusion, and I'm pretty sure

Thomas and I just added to it, but still, I feel strangely calm—even after having witnessed Zachary fall to the ground with a gunshot wound days prior.

"You ready?"

I stop at the sound of Brantley's voice. My pulse skyrockets when I see him leaning against the far wall in his dark jeans and black tee, with a hot smirk.

"For?" I take a hesitant step toward him.

"For me to introduce you to the Rebels."

I raise a brow. "I recall you all but banishing me from this school, and now you want your friends to meet me? What happened to worrying about your father finding out who I am?"

Brantley's dark chuckle sends a tingle down my spine. He looks so nonchalant with his hands in his pockets and casual shrug. "I've decided you're just another Rebel girl we have to watch out for."

I try to hide my disappointment. "Rebel girl? There were others before me?"

Brantley wastes no time erasing the space separating us. A fast breath tumbles out of my mouth when he pulls me in close. "There was no one before you *or* after you."

The confusion follows me all the way down the hall. I let him pull me through a door, and when darkness erupts around us, his hand tightens in mine. "You're the only one I've ever felt this way about. I was just too young to understand it when I left you in that closet."

I was too.

The longer Brantley pulls me by the hand, the harder my heart beats. I hear faint music and laughter, and it isn't until we're halfway through a door that I realize we're in the basement of St. Mary's.

I blink until I can focus and let my eyes adjust to the colorful lights blinking against stone walls. I ping-pong my attention around the vast area and skip past every set of eyes looking at me.

Four girls descend on me like I'm prey, and Brantley throws me right to the wolves without any warning.

His hand falls away, and my mouth opens to protest, but he winks, and I forget what I was going to say.

"Welcome to St. Mary's!" one of the girls says, while the other squeezes my hand.

"I'm Sloane. This is Mercedes. That's Journey, and–"

"I'm Gemma."

She's pretty, and I can tell she's genuine. When our hands touch in a brief handshake, I feel a weird sense of something warm. Like *family*.

"We're what they call the Rebel girls, and we wanna welcome you to your first claiming party."

Claiming party?

Journey snorts and rolls her eyes before walking away.

"Who decided that we're the *Rebel* girls?" Mercedes crosses her arms with clear agitation.

A tall guy swoops in the middle of our group. "I did. You got a problem with that?"

"As a matter of fact, Shiner…I do."

Suddenly, the lights turn off. I panic when I can't see Brantley, but that's when I feel a warm set of hands wrap around my waist. His front edges into my back, and when his lips touch the side of my neck, I grin.

"Are you ready to be claimed by a Rebel, baby?"

I bite my lip. *I'm more than ready.*

AFTERWORD

Did you love visiting the halls of St. Mary's Boarding School? If you haven't read the other books in the series, start with book one: **Good Girls Never Rise**

If you *have* read the other books in the series, then I want to say ***thank you so much*** for reading the series! It's always hard to end a world, especially one as detailed as St. Mary's and I am forever thankful for my loyal St. Mary's fans! There will always be a spot for you at St. Mary's and you're welcome back anytime. <3

Ps. I know you want more stories in this series! Make sure to check my webstite for upcoming news. I may have a few surprises up my sleeve!

sjsylvis.com

ALSO BY SJ SYLVIS

Bexley U Series

Weak Side

Ice Bet

Puck Block

Shadow Valley Series

Sticks and Stones

Untitled

English Prep Series

All the Little Lies

All the Little Secrets

All the Little Truths

St. Mary's Series

Good Girls Never Rise

Bad Boys Never Fall

Dead Girls Never Talk

Heartless Boys Never Kiss

Pretty Girls Never Lie

Standalones

Three Summers

Yours Truly, Cammie

Chasing Ivy

Falling for Fallon

Truth

ABOUT THE AUTHOR

S.J. Sylvis is an Amazon top 50 and USA Today bestselling author who is best known for her angsty new adult romances. She currently resides in Arizona with her husband, two small kiddos, and dog. She is obsessed with coffee, becomes easily attached to fictional characters, and spends most of her evenings buried in a book!

sjsylvis.com

ACKNOWLEDGMENTS

Thank you so much to every single reader who fell in love the St. Mary's Series! It is so bittersweet to end this world but the best thing about books is that you can always revisit the worlds within them. I hope I have created a place you can call home when you need some comfort! <3

I also want to thank every single person who has supported me thus far in my career! I have the worlds best family, friends, editors, proofers, graphic designers, PA, PR company, readers, etc.! It takes a village and **you are my village.**

xo

SJ